We were having a great day. But something was wrong.

At first I couldn't decide what. Then . . . when I looked at Richard I imagined putting my dad in his place. And me in Mary Anne's.

And maybe throw in a beach and some smog in the background.

My California homesickness was getting worse by the day. And it made me feel *so* guilty. I mean, I love my life in Stoneybrook, with my mum and my friends. Richard is always sweet to me. Mary Anne is the best sister I could imagine having.

So I didn't want to say anything. Everyone was having a fabulous time that day, and it wouldn't be right to burst the bubble.

"Dawn?" Mary Anne said gently. "What's wrong?"

"I want to go home!" The words just tumbled out of my mouth. I couldn't hold them back.

Fssssht! The bubble burst.

Other Babysitters to look out for:

Jessi and the Bad Babysitter
Get Well Soon, Mallory!
Stacey and the Cheerleaders

Babysitters Specials available:

Babysitters on Board!
Babysitters' Summer Holiday
Babysitters' Winter Holiday
Babysitters' Island Adventure
California Girls!
New York, New York!
Snowbound
Babysitters at Shadow Lake
Starring the Babysitters Club
Sea City, Here We Come!
The Babysitters Remember

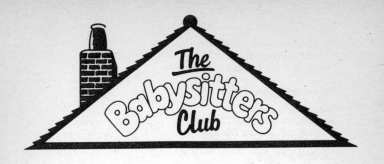

DAWN'S BIG MOVE

Ann M. Martin

Scholastic Children's Books,
7-9 Pratt Street, London NW1 0AE, UK
a division of Scholastic Publications Ltd
London ~ New York ~ Toronto ~ Sydney ~ Auckland

First published in the US by Scholastic Inc., 1993
First published in the UK by Scholastic Publications Ltd, 1995

Text copyright © Ann M. Martin, 1993
THE BABYSITTERS CLUB is a registered trademark of Scholastic Inc.

ISBN 0 590 13266 0

All rights reserved

Typeset in Plantin by Contour Typesetters, Southall, London
Printed by Cox & Wyman Ltd, Reading, Berks.

10 9 8 7 6 5 4 3 2 1

The author gratefully acknowledges
Peter Lerangis
for his help in
preparing this manuscript.

1st CHAPTER

"You add *what*?" asked my stepsister, Mary Anne. She looked up from the steaming wok on the kitchen stove.

"Arrowroot," I answered. "And keep stirring."

"*Arrowroot?*" Mary Anne said. "That sounds sickening."

"It's for thickening," I replied. Then I realized what I'd said. So I added, "Underthtand?"

We both started giggling. It was one of those days.

I don't know about you, but I go crazy in early autumn. Especially when the air's so cool and clear you can almost drink it. I just want to run around in the falling leaves and scream and sing. So what was I doing? Slaving in the kitchen with Mary Anne Spier, trying to make

1

"Tofu Garden Delight".

Bet you're dying to know what that is. Well, I wasn't too sure myself. But it's the name of this *excellent* stir-fry dish at a restaurant called The Source in Anaheim, California (that's close to where I'm from). As Mary Anne and I had agreed to make dinner that night, I was determined to puzzle out the recipe. Even if it meant being cooped up indoors on an incredible day.

You know what Mary Anne thinks? She's convinced I like autumn because in California the weather's the same all year round and there's no autumn. Well, I *love* Mary Anne—she's my best friend in the world and I mean the *world*—but here's news for all you East Coast dudes: *WRONG*. There *are* seasons in California, and leaves *do* fall from trees. Okay, it's not as *vivid* as here, or as *cold*, but it has its own good points.

Here, by the way, is Stoneybrook, Connecticut. And I, by the way, am Dawn Schafer. My mum and I moved here from California when I was in seventh grade (I'm in eighth now). You see, Mum grew up here and her parents still live here, so she decided to move back after she and my dad got divorced.

Yes, it's true. My parents live on opposite sides of the country, like bookends. Sometimes I tell people I've got a "bicoastal family" because it sounds pretty cool. But let me tell you, it *feels* pretty awful.

You know what else? My brother, Jeff, lives in California with my dad. He did move here originally with Mum and me, but he wasn't happy at all. He started having trouble at school and being really moody, and eventually we realized he was homesick for Dad (and California). So after a lot of arguing and crying, my parents decided to let him live with Dad. I really, really, *really* miss him. He's ten years old, and I don't know, I feel weird not being with him to see him grow up. I've been thinking about visiting Dad and Jeff again a *lot* lately.

I have been out there a few times. It's fun, but boy, is it hard to say goodbye! Also, my dad has this girlfriend called Carol, which makes things complicated. At first I didn't care for Carol. Okay, the truth is *I couldn't stand her*. She was always trying to act super-young, as if she could be my age, but she's about *thirty-two*! Actually, I don't mind her now. She acted her age once, and I was pretty impressed. I mean it, too. It happened when the whole Babysitters Club went out there on a visit. (The BSC's a club I belong to. I'll tell you about it later.) One of our members, Stacey McGill, got a crush on some guy and started hanging around with him and his friends. Well, they were pretty wild—wild enough to end up having a car accident. Nobody was hurt, thank goodness. But when Carol found out, instead of keeping it a secret (to be cool and get on our good side), she told my dad. I know it may sound weird, but I respected her after that. She was acting like a responsible grown-up.

Dad's thinking of marrying Carol, and that's another reason I want to go out there so badly. I mean, if she's going to be his wife (my *stepmother*) I should get to know her a little, shouldn't I?

Anyway, that's the western side of my family. As for me and my mum, well, we haven't exactly let the grass grow under our feet. (Don't you love that expression? It means that we haven't just sat around doing nothing.) First of all, I joined the Babysitters Club. Because of that, I made eight fantastic friends, including Mary Anne Spier. And Mum's got involved with all kinds of local organizations. She also got involved with a *guy*! Who? Well, he was her high-school sweetheart and his name's Richard Spier.

Yes, the father of Mary Anne, who, as you know, became my stepsister! You see, Mary Anne's mum died when she was a baby. Mary Anne doesn't even remember her, and Richard didn't talk about her at all for years. Her death left him shocked and heartbroken, and he could hardly make it through the day. He even left Mary Anne with her grandparents for a long time, until he could pull himself together. Eventually he took her back and brought her up by himself. Now, he's not exactly Mr Laid Back. With Mary Anne, he became incredibly strict. He made her wear little-girl clothes, keep her hair in plaits, and come in for super-early curfews until *seventh grade*. Mary Anne hated that, but she forgives him. She says he was just worried about being a perfect mother *and* father.

Whatever.

Luckily, he treats her like a real thirteen-year-old now. He's still rather stuffy, and super-organized. (Make that mega-organized. *Turbo*-organized. I mean, he wears his shirts in a strict order each day so they wear out evenly.) But my mum liberated him. Now, how would you picture a woman who'd fall in love with Richard Spier? Guess again. My mum couldn't be more different. She's . . . well, easy-going, fun-loving, carefree, absent-minded. . . .

She does do some pretty strange things. In our house, it's not unusual to find a mitten in the fridge or keys in the microwave. And it's quite amazing that we manage to eat proper dinners. Once I discovered raisins in my clam chowder. Another time she made a yoghurt-based salad dressing with oregano and ground pepper—but we had to throw it away because she used vanilla-flavoured yoghurt.

Ta-da! We're now on one of my favourite topics. Food. I'm very careful about what I put in my body. I eat no red meat, and I find sugary things absolutely disgusting. Whole grains, sprouts, tofu, organic vegetables—I love natural, healthy foods.

Okay. Have you finished saying "Ugh!" and pretending to throw up? Good. A lot of kids feel the same way, but you know what? I'm shrugging. It doesn't matter to me. That's the way I am, and I'm quite happy about it.

"Here it is!" I exclaimed, pulling a jar of arrowroot out of the cupboard. (It's a white powder that looks like baking soda.)

"What does it taste like?" Mary Anne asked. "Wood?"

"No, Mary Anne," I replied patiently. "I mean, not that I *know* what wood tastes like. Arrowroot's like cornflour, but not as gloppy. Now *keep stirring*! Look, the *bok choy's* burning."

"The who?"

My stepsister, you may have noticed, isn't a health food freak. But I love her anyway. Of all the people I've ever met,

6

she's the most caring and sensitive. She can almost read my mind when I'm feeling terrible, and she's a really good listener. I'm *so* lucky to have Mary Anne as a sister. The only thing I don't like doing with her is going to the cinema. She cries a lot in general, but in the cinema it's pretty embarrassing. I mean, when we saw *Pocketful of Miracles* at an oldies festival once, they nearly had to call a flood warning.

I should also tell you that Mary Anne's the *only* BSC member with a steady boyfriend. His name's Logan Bruno and his looks are *número uno*. We're talking hunk here. He's got curly hair, blue eyes, a Southern accent, and he plays sports and likes babysitting.

No, he's not perfect. He can be bossy (Mary Anne broke up with him over that once) and he takes it too personally when his sports friends tease him about his babysitting. But apart from that, he's pretty cool.

Now. Back to the drama of the stir-fried dinner. Act One, the Preparation. I threw in some vinegar and soy sauce and it began to smell delicious. Even Mary Anne agreed. I checked the rice, and it was perfect.

Mary Anne made the dressing for the salad we'd prepared (with a homemade, *plain*-yoghurt base), and we were ready for . . .

Act Two. It began with the ringing of the doorbell and the opening of the front door. "What smells so *fabulous*?"

Enter my mum, Sharon Porter Schafer Spier. Wearing a summery-print oversized blouse and matching shorts, she breezed into the kitchen and gave her daughter and stepdaughter a kiss. "What a treat to come home to dinner!" she exclaimed.

She exited.

A few minutes later Richard Spier arrived, and immediately laid the table. (Forks and knives for him and Mary Anne, chopsticks for Mum and me.)

Act Three. Dinner.

Theme: Health food can taste good.

"My compliments to the chefs," Richard said.

"What's your secret?" Mum asked.

"The different textures," I explained.

"And the right amount of arrowroot," Mary Anne added.

Richard stopped chewing. "What?"

Mary Anne gave me a look. We both started laughing.

"Just eat, dear," Mum said with a smile.

Richard shrugged and munched. Before long we were all jabbering away. Well, not all. Richard doesn't jabber. He *speaks*, slowly and clearly. But even he was pretty excited about something. You could see it in his eyes. It was the look he gets when he's got something to say about the stock market (zzzzz). But this time it was actually about something interesting.

"I was reading in the Stamford paper about the joint fund-raising event by the Chambers of Commerce of Stoneybrook and Lawrenceville," he said. (Hang on, it gets better.) "This, er, 'Run for Your Money', I believe it's called. It looks interesting. Anyone can enter a team— colleagues, families, friends—and there are all kinds of crazy events. You pay a fee to enter and the proceeds go to charities. I think Stoneybrook's donating to an organization for the homeless, and Lawrenceville's chosen a literacy pro- gramme."

"I wonder if Kristy knows about this?" Mary Anne said.

"She's probably already put us into teams," I said.

"Wouldn't it be fun to get some of the little kids involved?" Mary Anne asked.

"Well, I was thinking that the four of us should enter something," Richard suggested.

Mum raised her eyebrows in surprise. (Richard isn't exactly athletic.)

Neither is Mary Anne. "I don't know, Dad," she said.

Richard stood up and pulled the newspaper out of his briefcase, which was lying by the wall. "Look, most of the events aren't strictly speaking sports competitions. For example, sack races—"

"'There are sideshows,'" Mum began reading, "'tug-of-war, pie-eating contests, underwear race—'"

"Underwear race?" Mary Anne said, blushing. (Yes, *blushing*.)

"That's the one we should enter!" I piped up.

Now it was Richard's turn to raise an eyebrow.

"I think it would be fun to enter as a family!" Mum said.

"Yes, it would," Mary Anne replied.

I nodded. I know I should have been more excited, but when Mum said "as a family" I thought of Jeff and Dad. They would *love* to be in "Run for Your Money". They're both athletic, and they've got a great sense of humour.

And I realized again I was *dying* to see them.

"Dawn?" Mary Anne said. "Is something wrong?"

"Uh-uh," I answered. "I was just . . . thinking. You know, about Jeff and Dad."

Then I made myself smile and chopsticked some dinner into my mouth.

Mum looked at me sympathetically. "Why don't you phone them tonight?"

"Yes, I think I will," I said. I chewed on some *bok choy* for a minute. "Mum? Would it be too expensive for me to go out and see them?"

Mum looked at Richard, who shrugged. "Well, we can book some tickets for Thanksgiving," Mum said.

"Okay," I replied. "That would be great."

I tried to sound happy, but I know I didn't. Thanksgiving was *months* away.

"Unfortunately, it's the nearest school holiday," Richard added.

"I know . . ." I mumbled.

"You really miss them, don't you?" Mary Anne said.

My eyes started to fill with tears. *My* eyes. The ones belonging to me, Dawn Schafer, who teases Mary Anne about crying like a tap at the cinema.

"I know how you feel," Mum said. "Look, Thanksgiving's not that far away. But I suppose we *could* try to arrange a long weekend before then, if you're desperate to see them."

"No," I said, "that's okay. I can wait."

I dug into my Tofu Garden Delight. I

11

had a great need to stuff my mouth. If I didn't, I might blurt out that I was lying.

I did phone home that night. Jeff answered the phone.

"Hi," I said. "It's your sister."

"Oh, no!"

I ignored the snide remark. "How's it going?"

"Fine."

"Is school okay?"

"Yuck!"

"Too bad."

"Guess what? In gym I won the home run derby. And guess what else? I came fifth in the physical fitness contest, but that was out of a hundred and three kids. And I got an O on my book report. That's for Outstanding. It's like an A in the older grades. Or better."

Typical Jeff. He'll tell you everything eventually, but he won't answer a direct question.

"That's fantastic! And how's Dad?"

"Good."

I took a breath. "And Carol?"

"What about her?"

"Well . . . is Dad still going out with her?"

"Yeah."

He didn't sound too thrilled. "Jeff, are you being nice to her?"

"*Yes*," he said, in a way that meant *no*.

I just had to ask the next question. "Has Dad said anything about marrying her yet?"

"No. Do you want to talk to him? He's right here."

"Okay."

After a moment Dad came on the phone. "Hi, Sunshine!"

"Hi, Dad. I miss you."

"I miss you, too. We've just got back from roller-skating on the beach. Jeff's getting too fast for me."

"Oh, I wish I could come out and see you!"

"Well, Thanksgiving's just around the corner."

Yes, a *far* corner, I thought. "Uh-huh."

We talked a little more. Carol was there, so she came on the phone for a bit.

When the conversation was over, I went to my room and looked out of the window. The leaves on the old maple were starting to turn yellow.

I narrowed my eyes and tried to imagine it was a palm tree.

2nd CHAPTER

RRRRRINNGG!

Horrors. It was 5:28 on a Friday afternoon. Starting time for our Babysitters Club meeting was still two minutes away, but the phone was already ringing.

"Boy, are we popular!" Claudia Kishi said. She picked up the receiver. "Hello, Babysitters Club. . . Oh, hi, Mrs Papadakis . . . A week from Saturday at eleven? Er, let me find out."

She looked at Mary Anne, who was checking the record book. "Jessi, Kristy and Stacey are free," Mary Anne said.

"I can't," Jessi Ramsey informed her. "I'm going away."

"I'll do it," Kristy volunteered. (Which made sense, because Kirsty lives right opposite the Papadakises.)

"Kristy'll be there," Claudia said into

the phone. "Great. Okay, 'bye."

There. You've just seen the BSC at work. Simple, isn't it? Parents phone us, we arrange sitting jobs. There are seven full-time members (and two associates), so someone's always available. Well, almost always.

Our headquarters is Claudia's bedroom, because she's the only one of us who has her own phone with her own number. (Claud's the club vice-chairman.) We meet on Mondays, Wednesdays and Fridays, from five-thirty to six. Most of our business comes from regular clients, but new parents phone us, too. They hear about us from other parents, or they see one of the posters we sometimes put up around town.

Want to know why the Babysitters Club's so successful? Two words: Kristy Thomas. She thought up the idea for the BSC one day when her mum was having trouble finding a sitter. The club started with just Kristy, Claudia and Mary Anne, but the idea worked so well they had to expand.

We all have titles and duties, like a company. Kristy, of course, is our chairman. She runs the meetings and thinks up brilliant ideas, such as the record book (which I'll explain later) and the notebook, in which we write about each sitting job. Writing in the notebook is rather a pain, but

15

it's helpful to read about how other sitters have solved problems with certain kids. (Also, some of the entries are really funny.)

Kid-Kits are another patented Kristy idea. They're boxes filled with old games, toys and books—basically stuff we've found lying around our houses. Sounds boring? Well, kids don't think so. They absolutely *adore* Kid-Kits. Only Kristy could have thought of that. Her brain's so crammed full of ideas, sometimes words just come spilling out of her mouth before she can think. (That's a nice way of saying she can be loud and bossy.)

Guess who's best friends with Kristy the Great and Powerful? Mary Anne the Shy and Meek. They've known each other since they were in nappies. Actually, they look rather alike. Both are on the short side (Kristy's shorter), and both have dark brown hair and brown eyes. But there the similarities end. Kristy's very athletic. Mary Anne practically breaks out in a rash if you mention the word *gym*. Mary Anne's style of dress is neat and college-girl style. Kristy's style is super-casual and down-to-earth—jeans, T-shirts, trainers. And that style didn't change one bit after she became rich.

No, she didn't win the national lottery. Her mum married this millionaire named

Watson Brewer. You see, Kristy grew up across the street from Claudia in a normal, non-rich house. She's got two older brothers called Charlie and Sam. When her younger brother, David Michael, was born, her dad left. Talk about thoughtless! Well, Mrs Thomas did a fantastic job bringing up kids *and* working full-time. Then she met Watson and—*whoosh!*—off went the Thomas family to live in a mansion. I'm serious, that place is huge. Now it's also pretty crowded. Watson's got two kids from his first marriage (Karen and Andrew), who live there on alternate weekends. Then there's Emily Michelle, an adopted Vietnamese girl. Kristy's grandmother, Nannie, lives there to help run the house, which includes looking after all the pets.

Kristy lives on the other side of town now, so her brother Charlie has to drive her to meetings. He always gets her there on time. Kristy's *extremely* punctual, and Charlie knows enough to stay on her good side.

"This meeting will come to order!" Kristy announced as the clock by Claudia's bed turned to 5:30. "Any new business to discuss?"

"Yes," Claudia said. "I've made an important discovery." She ran to her

17

wardrobe and disappeared behind a very full clothes rail.

Mallory Pike gasped. "Uh-oh, a secret world. Like the one in *The Lion, the Witch and the Wardrobe*."

No such luck. Claudia emerged holding two huge bags that said "Holiday M&M's", decorated in green, silver and red. "Ta-da!"

"But those are from *last winter*!" Kristy said.

"So?" Claudia replied. "Chocolate doesn't go off."

I should explain something. Claudia Kishi lives for junk food. She thinks the four food groups are sweets, crisps, pretzels and popcorn. If I ever invited her over for Tofu Garden Delight, she'd turn blue and faint. Honestly, I don't know how she stays healthy. And guess what? She's got a fabulous figure and her skin doesn't even have the slightest hint of a blemish.

To tell you the truth, Claudia could probably be a model. She's Japanese-American, and she's got the most gorgeous almond-shaped eyes and silky black hair. She also has *style* with a capital S. She can throw together trendy bargain-basement clothes and look *so* cool.

How someone so stylish can live in such a pigsty of a room is beyond me. There are clothes all over the place. She's an excellent artist too, so here's what else is lying around: easels, poster board, jewellery-making tools, paints and brushes, markers, sketch paper and plaster of Paris. Not to mention Hula Hoops, Yorkie bars, pretzels, Milky Bars and crisps. Claud's room is like a junk food *Where's Wally?* Her parents are strict about good nutrition and fine literature, so Claudia has to hide all her junk food *and* her Nancy Drew mysteries (she's addicted to them, too). She pulls them out from between sweaters, under her bed, inside shoes, *everywhere*. So it's no surprise that she sometimes loses track of things, like the holiday M&M's.

How do we fit in Claud's room? She manages to shove everything away before meetings. (If she didn't, Kristy would probably nag her for ever.)

Anyway, so there we were in Claud's room. Most of us were popping red and green M&M's into our mouths and getting into the holiday spirit about three months early (or nine months late). But not Stacey McGill and me. However, being a very thoughtful person, Claudia had squirrelled away some sesame crackers for us.

No, Stacey's not on a diet. Neither is she a health-food fan like I am. She's got diabetes, which means her body can't control the level of sugar in her blood. If she ate too many chocolate bars she could end up in hospital. Every day she has to give herself injections of something called insulin. Can you imagine?

Like me, Stacey moved to Stoneybrook permanently a year after her parents got divorced. Also, like me, she's blonde (although a darker shade). Apart from that, we're pretty different. Her clothes are cool and sophisticated (mine are more casual). And she's extra-clever at maths (I'm not).

The maths part is the reason why Stacey became our club treasurer. She collects subs from us every Monday and puts them in our official treasury (an old manila envelope). Subs are the only *bad* thing about the BSC, but they're necessary. They help pay Claud's phone bill and Charlie Thomas's driving fee. They also buy supplies for Kid-Kits, and pizza for us (if there's a surplus).

Stacey grew up in New York City. I don't know how she did it. The last time I visited I was too scared to leave the flat I was staying in. I was convinced I'd be mugged, flattened by a falling brick, or attacked by an army of giant cockroaches. Well, somehow Stace lived her life there and turned out pretty normal. After moving to Stoneybrook, her family actually moved *back* to NYC (both moves were because of her dad's job). That was when her parents got divorced, and she and her mum moved back here.

I'm so glad Stace is in the BSC. She's easy to talk to, and she's the only member who understands what divorce feels like. But I have to admit I envy her sometimes. She's only a short train ride away from *her* dad.

"Er, Jessi," Mary Anne said after carefully swallowing her M&M's. "Did you say you were going away?"

"Oh. Yes," Jessi replied. "I'm going to Oakley this weekend to visit Keisha." (Oakley is where Jessi grew up, and Keisha's her cousin.)

"That's great," Claudia said. "You haven't been back for—"

"Months!" Jessi was smiling so hard I thought her cheeks would pop. "I'm so excited. I can't wait to see Keisha, and I'm going to try to see some of my friends. I'm dying to visit my old ballet school, too. My teacher's going to be shocked to see me."

Mary Anne was entering Jessi's trip in the BSC record book, in her neat handwriting. She's the club secretary, which is a really difficult job. She keeps track of our sitting schedules, making sure to remember all our other commitments—doctor's and dentist's appointments, ballet classes and after-school activities. She also has to update our client list regularly, complete with current rates of pay (they vary from client to client.) On top of *that* she keeps a detailed description of the likes and dislikes of all our charges.

Know how many mistakes she's made? None. And knowing her, she probably never will.

Jessi, by the way, is really into ballet. You should see her perform. Incredible! She practically glides in the air. She takes lessons in Stamford and has danced major roles in various productions. One day she's going to be a professional dancer. And you heard it here first.

I can't mention Jessi without mentioning Mallory Pike. They're best friends, and our junior members. *Junior* because they're eleven and in sixth grade, two years younger than the rest of us. They both have early curfews, so they mainly take afternoon jobs. Here's what they have in common: they love reading (especially horse books), they're convinced their parents treat them like babies, they're the oldest kids in their families and they're extremely creative. Mallory's talents are writing and illustrating. She wants to be a children's book author one day.

Here's what they don't have in common:

Jessi's black and Mal's white, Mal wears glasses and a brace (Jessi doesn't) and Jessi's got a *much* smaller family than Mal's. There are eight Pike kids altogether (yes, *eight*). Jessi only has two siblings: an eight-year-old sister called Becca and a baby brother called John Philip Ramsey, Jr (Squirt, for short).

We've got two associate members, Logan Bruno (yes, Mary Anne's boyfriend) and Shannon Kilbourne. They're our backups when we get busy. They don't come to most meetings, but they're both *excellent* sitters. Shannon's the only member who doesn't go to SMS. She goes to a private school, Stoneybrook Day School.

Then there's me. I'm the alternate member. That means I take over whenever anyone can't get to a meeting. I became the club treasurer when Stacey moved back to New York. (Was I glad she came back to Stoneybrook!)

Back to the meeting. The more Jessi talked about seeing her old friends, the more my heart sank. Don't get me wrong. I was glad she was so excited, but it made me think of *my* old friends in California.

Then Stacey talked about how much *she* loves visiting *her* old friends.

I kept picturing a map of the United States in my head. I saw a dot marked

STONEYBROOK with three lines sticking out from it. One short line connected it to New York City, another short one connected it to Oakley, New Jersey—and an incredibly long one stretched all the way to my dad's house in Palo City, California.

"You two are lucky to be so close to your old neighbourhoods," I eventually said. "I miss mine so much."

Clunk. That stopped the conversation flat.

Kristy spoke first. "Well, what can you do about it?"

Change the subject, that's what. And hope that one day Kristy would invent a magic carpet or something. "Oh, I'm going there for Thanksgiving," I replied with a shrug. Then I said, "Anyone read about 'Run for Your Money'?"

"Our family's already signed up!" Kristy said.

"I've read that athletics can harm your health," Claudia remarked, stuffing a Hula Hoop in her mouth. "But we're going to go anyway. Probably just to watch Janine win all the IQ games." (Claudia's sister, Janine, is a certified genius.)

"I hope they'll have pinball machines," Mallory said.

"I hope they'll have foosball," Stacey added.

24

Claudia looked at her. "What?"

"You know, a table with these long poles attached to players, who kick a ball when you rotate the pole."

"Table football!" Mallory said.

"Whatever," Stacey replied.

"Well, you can all cheer me and Charlie in the three-legged race," Kristy added.

It turned out all my friends' families were going to enter. That was cool. It gave me something to look forward to in the long trudge towards Thanksgiving.

3rd
CHAPTER

"Oh, this is ridiculous!" Richard was struggling with the zip on his trousers. "And where am I supposed to drop this?"

None of us could answer. We were *sick* with laughter, sprawled out on the grass in our back garden.

It was Saturday morning, and we were practising for "Run for Your Money". Now, if you told me an alien had landed in my back garden, I *probably* wouldn't believe you. But if you told me Richard Spier would agree to take part in an underwear race in "Run for Your Money", I'd think you were crazy.

Well, that was exactly what Mum had managed to do—persuade Richard. Don't ask me how. She had even bought him a tank top undershirt and an outsize pair of boxer shorts with red hearts on them, just for the occasion.

The hearts were showing through his trousers, which made us laugh even more, and his belly was jiggling under his undershirt.

"I'm really not sure about this . . ." Richard was now hopping on one foot, trying to pull his trousers over his big, clunky shoes. His face was redder than the hearts.

"You look so *sweet*, Richard!" Mum blurted out, still clutching her stomach.

She was wearing lightweight long johns. I was down to a two-piece swimsuit. Mary Anne was wearing a modest one-piece with a skirt.

I should probably explain. In an underwear race you peel off your clothes as you run. The first person to get to the finishing line in his or her underwear wins. (It doesn't have to be actual underwear. Mum says people sometimes wear outrageous things. It's the spirit that counts—the spirit of silliness and fun.)

"Oh, honestly, I give up," Richard eventually said in a huff. He was standing there in his heart boxer pants, with his trousers round his ankles and his clodhopper shoes poking out. We were *screaming*. We couldn't help it.

Richard wasn't amused. He started trying to walk back to the house—and you can imagine what that looked like.

That was when he gave up. He just sat on the ground and started chuckling. "You don't suppose there's another event we might try to enter instead?" he asked.

"*No!*" Mary Anne and I replied.

"*Wait!*" said Mum. "What about tug-of-war? We've got a rope, haven't we?"

"Oooh, great!" Mary Anne said.

"I'll get it," I volunteered.

As I ran into the barn, Richard stood and began pulling up his trousers in a hurry. So fast, in fact, that he pushed the heart boxer shorts up so that they bunched over the top of his belt.

I found a rope on the barn wall, grabbed it and ran out. "How should we do this?" I asked.

"Girls against boys," Mum said.

Richard looked at her blankly. "Girls against—"

"Or is that going to be too tough for you, dear?"

"Too tough? We'll see about that!" Richard took one end of the rope and walked away from us, his boxer shorts billowing over the top of his trousers.

I don't know how we kept from cracking

up. Instead, we all dug in until the line was taut.

"Ready?" Mum announced. "Set? Go!"

"Wait, I—" Richard seemed suddenly uncomfortable about something, but it was too late. We girls had already begun pulling.

Richard pulled back. He's stronger than I thought. His biceps were bulging.

It was unfair, I know. We'd caught him off guard. And there *were* three of us. He began staggering forward, losing his balance. And it soon became clear why he'd been uncomfortable. His trousers were slipping down again.

"Heave . . . *ho!*" Mum grunted. We gave a strong yank, and—*whomp!*—down went poor Richard.

He landed on his hands and knees, his trousers down around his thighs.

"Mr Spier?"

We all turned to see Marilyn and Carolyn Arnold staring at Richard. They're identical twins who live around the corner from us. They were dressed in tennis whites, on their way home from a lesson. Their parents were behind them, gently nudging them forward. I could tell the grown-ups were trying hard not to laugh.

Well, you've never seen a grown man spring to his feet faster. He pulled himself together, trying to look nonchalant. "Hello, there!" he called out. "The girls are giving me a real workout. This 'Run for Your Money' is quite a lot of fun."

Oh, was his face red! Mr Arnold nodded and said, "Yes. Looks like it. Maybe we'll enter, too."

Carolyn Arnold shot a glance at her father. "We will?"

"Er, come on. It's almost lunchtime," Mrs Arnold said to her daughters.

"Well, see you later!" Mr Arnold called. "Have fun!"

"Oh, we will! Ha, ha!" Richard replied, with a very forced laugh.

Mary Anne was giving her dad a sympathetic look. "Are you okay?" she asked.

Richard raised one eyebrow. "I've got an idea. A family wrestling match—*boys against girls*!"

"Aaaaaagh!" we screamed, giggling like crazy as he tore after us. For a few minutes we all dodged him. I could tell he was loosening up and having a good time.

Before long we all collapsed on the ground, panting. Mum nuzzled up against Richard, who gave her a kiss on the forehead. Then he looked at Mary Anne with a fond smile and put his arm around her shoulders. "I expect the Arnolds will be trying to move to another neighbourhood soon," he remarked. "To get away from their weird neighbours."

Mum and Mary Anne laughed. They both looked happy. Richard looked happy, too.

Me? I was staring at the grass. I *wasn't* feeling happy. I should have been. It was a gorgeous day, warm and summery. We were having a great time. But something was wrong.

At first I couldn't decide what. Then a weird memory popped into my head. It was a TV show I'd seen, about how computers could completely change photographs by replacing images. For instance, you could put yourself into a photo from the Civil War.

Well, when I looked at Richard I imagined putting my dad in his place. And me in Mary Anne's.

And maybe throw in a beach and some smog in the background.

My California homesickness was getting worse by the day. And it made me feel *so* guilty. I mean, I love my life in Stoneybrook, with my mum and my friends. Richard is always sweet to me. Mary Anne is the best sister I could imagine having.

So I didn't want to say anything. Everyone was having a fabulous time that day, and it wouldn't be right to burst the bubble.

"Dawn?" Mary Anne said gently. "What's wrong?"

"I want to go home!" The words just tumbled out of my mouth. I couldn't hold them back.

Fsssssht! The bubble burst. Richard's smile faded, and he glanced at Mum. Mary Anne shifted herself so she could sit next to me.

I hung my head lower and played with a few strands of grass.

"You've been thinking about your dad and Jeff a lot lately," Mary Anne said.

I nodded. I could hardly force the word "Yes" out.

Mum sighed. "Well, I suppose I should phone Dad and work out a good weekend for a visit. It'll be hard to get tickets, you know—"

"I don't mean *go back*, like, go back for a weekend," I interrupted. "I mean really go back. To stay. For six months or so."

"Six months?" Mum looked shocked.

Even I was surprised at what I'd said. But it was true. I just hadn't wanted to admit it. Not even to myself.

My stomach was churning. Not to mention my brain. I had no idea what was going to come out of my mouth now. "I—I just miss my old life, Mum. I can't help it. I miss my friends, the weather . . . but mostly I miss Dad and Jeff. I mean, I've been living away from them for so long."

"I thought you liked it here," Mum protested.

"I do! I *love* it. But I've got two families. I love my Stoneybrook family. Really. But I love my California family, too."

"And you want equal time," Mum said.

"Well, I don't know about *equal*—"

"Then what do you mean?"

"I don't *know* what I mean! I just want to be with them, that's all."

I couldn't believe it. Mum looked hurt, almost angry.

Richard spoke up. "I can understand your feelings, Dawn," he said. "It must be hard to be split between your parents."

"But what about school?" Mum barged on. "You'll have to register in a new place, and start in the middle of the year—"

"Yes, very difficult to do," Richard said in a soft voice. "Obviously this is something we need to think carefully about."

"That's okay," I said. "I don't want to upset everybody."

Mum sighed and shook her head. "I don't mean to sound so negative, darling. It's just that—well, it was so hard to see Jeff go back. And now you . . . I—I've tried my best. Is something bothering you here, something we might be able to sort out?"

"Oh, Mum, it's not *you*," I replied.

"Of course it's not," Richard said, giving Mum a hug.

"Okay." Mum was trying very hard to smile.

I felt really awful. I didn't think Mum would take it so personally. "Well, I know the arrangements would be a lot of work," I said, "and if it's too much, I'll understand." (You don't know how hard it was for me to say those words.)

"Let me think about it, darling," Mum replied. "I can tell how much you want to go."

Mary Anne hadn't said a word through all of this. I looked at her and realized why. She'd been trying not to cry.

"Oh, Mary Anne," I said. "I'm not going for ever."

"I . . ." *Sniff, sniff.* "I know. I'm sorry. I—I want you to be happy, Dawn. Really. It's just that if you go I'll miss you so m—" *Sniff, sniff. "Much!"*

"Well, dears, it's still a big if," Mum said.

Richard got up. "Why don't we try that tug-of-war again, then go and get some pizza for lunch?"

"Great idea," I said.

Mary Anne wiped her eyes. "Okay."

Mum walked to the rope and picked it up. She was smiling at me. I think it was the saddest smile I've ever seen.

4th CHAPTER

Saturday

Kristy, I dont know how you do it. I mean, organising kids, like with Kristys' Crushers. Its so hard. Well, anyway, I tryed to do it today. I sat for Jammie and Lucy Newton, and it seemd like a perfict day to practis for Run for Youre Money. Well all I can say is I am so glad I had some help. If I didnt, I think Ild have collap colapsed er pased out...

"Ba ba ba ba ba ba ba," said Lucy Newton, looking up at Claudia.

"Oops! Here's your baba," Claudia replied, gently reinserting a bottle that had fallen from Lucy's mouth.

"Seven!" Jamie Newton called out. "Did you see me, Claudia? Seven!"

"Mm-hm," Claudia said, smiling. "Great, Jamie.

Jamie was perched on his bike with stabilizers. He'd just completed his seventh round trip on the Newtons' drive—his seventh *very* slow round trip.

It was early Saturday afternoon. Several blocks away, the Drama of Homesick Dawn was going strong. But at the Newtons' house, Claudia was having a peaceful time, sitting for two of our oldest charges.

Maybe *oldest* isn't the right word. Jamie's four and Lucy's not even one. What I mean is, the Newton kids were among our *first* charges. In fact, Kristy, Claudia and Mary Anne sat for Jamie before Lucy was born (and before the BSC was invented).

"Eight!" Jamie shouted.

"Great," Claudia said.

"I didn't fall!"

"I know."

"Are you watching?"

"*Yes.*"

Claudia's patient, kind and cheerful. But even Claudia has her limits.

She was going crazy.

She unfolded a copy of the *Stoneybrook News*, which was full of articles about "Run for Your Money". She tried to read it, but Jamie screamed out a new number in the middle of each sentence.

At "Thirteen!" Claudia had her big idea.

She remembered that Stacey was sitting for Charlotte Johanssen nearby, and that Jessi and Mal were at the Pikes' house. "Run for Your Money" would be a perfect excuse to get them together (and get Jamie off the bike). She guessed a lot of families would be entering, so everyone could do with some practice.

"I'll be right back!" Claudia called out, rushing inside with Lucy. "Stay away from the road!" As she made her phone calls, Jamie charged ahead to Round Trip Eighteen.

Well, Jessi, Mal and Stacey all *loved* the idea. Claudia felt so relieved, she decided to reward herself. So she took a Milky Way from her shoulder bag and tossed it into the Newtons' freezer. She planned to enjoy the FMW (frozen Milky Way) that night.

By the time Stacey, Charlotte and Becca came charging up the drive, Jamie was on his thirty-ninth round trip, and Claud was on a sun lounger, busily reading about the rules and events in "Run for Your Money". (Lucy had had enough. She was asleep in an outdoor cot.)

"Forty!" Jamie said. "Forty times up and down the drive!"

"Yea, Jamie!" Stacey cheered.

Don't encourage him! was what Claudia wanted to say. But she didn't. "Er, do you lot feel like practising for this 'Run for Your Money' thing?" (Okay, not exactly inspiring, but Claud's not an athlete.)

"*Yeeeeahh!*" Char and Becca cried.

"No-o-o-o!" Jamie protested.

"Can Becca and I run a three-legged race?" Charlotte wanted to know.

"*A three-legged race?*" Jamie said. He looked horrified—but interested.

"Of course!" Claudia said. "Come here, Jamie. I'll explain it."

Success. Jamie decided to join in. Stacey ran into the Newton house to get some rope. Becca and Charlotte grinned at Lucy.

And that was when a herd of wildebeests stampeded up the drive.

Well, that's what it sounded like. Actually, it was Jessi, Mal and the Pike kids. But that's nine people altogether. Nine *loud* people.

"HI!" they called.

"*Waaaaah!*" Lucy shrieked.

"I've found some rope!" Stacey shouted cheerfully, from the doorway.

"Oooh, a bike!" said Claire Pike, climbing on to Jamie's two-wheeler.

"*Nooooooo!*" Jamie roared. He ran to Claire and pushed her off.

"Owwwwww!" Claire cried.

It took some serious babysitting skills to clear up this situation. Claudia fed Lucy, Stacey separated Jamie and Claire, and Jessi and Mal kept the rest of the Pikes out of trouble.

(As I mentioned before, Mal has seven siblings. There are ten-year-old triplets—Adam, Byron and Jordan. Then there's Vanessa, who's nine. She wants to be a poet, so she likes to speak in rhyme. Nicky's eight, but wants desperately to be ten like his brothers. Next is seven-year-old Margo, followed by Claire, who's five.)

At last, when everyone was quiet, Claudia said, "Okay, there are a lot of events to choose from. You'll all be in the same team. In each event, a team from Stoneybrook plays against a team from Lawrenceville, okay?"

40

"The whole *team* ties their legs together?" Nicky asked.

"That's hard," Margo said.

Adam groaned. "I think you lot must have taken *moron* pills this morning."

"Listen to me," Claudia replied. "In something like the three-legged race, the officials will record the time it takes each pair to finish. Then they add up the times to find which *team* was fastest. Now, let's start by practising some events, then splitting into teams for a mock competition, okay?"

About halfway through the explanation, the kids began tying their legs together, in pairs: Adam-Jordan, Mal-Jessi, and Jamie-Claire (who became the Red team); and Byron-Nicky, Vanessa-Margo (who were the Blue team with Becca and Char). Stacey helped each pair tie one person's right leg to the other's left. (Adam and Jordan had refused help, and they ended up tying their right legs together.)

Claudia had the easy job. She sat in a sun lounger, held Lucy, and watched.

The kids began to practise. Jamie and Claire fell before they'd moved an inch. Mal and Jessi took it slowly, but Jessi kept pointing her toes, which made Mal giggle, so they collapsed. Char and Becca couldn't stay upright, so they decided to crawl. Byron and Nicky yelled at each other but

41

couldn't work out how to move. Adam and Jordan kept running around in circles, laughing their heads off.

Claudia was giggling so hard, she almost dropped Lucy.

The kids kept at it for a bit. Then they split into teams and held a race. Four pairs were actually able to reach the finishing line, in this order: Becca-Char (Blue), Adam-Jordan, Jessi-Mal (both Red), and Byron-Nicky (Blue).

Well, Jordan was furious. "You pushed in front of us!" he shouted at Becca and Char.

"No, we did not!" Becca replied.

"It's not fair," Bryon mumbled, his eyes filling with tears. "Jessi and Mal are *sitters*, not kids."

"Yeah!" Adam shouted. "I vote we do it again!"

"Hey, it's only a game," Stacey insisted.

"Er, let's move on to something else," Claudia said, frantically reading the newspaper article. "How about a . . . rolling race?"

This time the kids had to *roll* to the finishing line in pairs—holding hands, with heads pointed towards each other and feet pointing outwards. As the garden's quite small, they did it two pairs at a time. (Mal and Jessi tactfully stayed out of it.)

You can imagine what that was like. Byron and Nicky rolled into the Newtons' flowerbeds and squashed three flowers. Becca and Charlotte rolled into each other. Jamie and Claire managed to knock over the bike and get into another fight.

In the middle of the practice, Mrs Barrett walked past with her three kids. Immediately the older ones, Buddy and Suzi, replaced Jessi and Mal on the Red team.

After a few tries, most of the kids eventually mastered the rolling. Stacey organized them into races, and Adam and Jordan won. They were the fastest.

"It's not fair!" Margo shouted. "They're bigger!"

"Yeah," Nicky said. "We should get a handicap."

"But you'll be racing in the same team," Stacey reminded them. "This is only a practice."

"Er, how about the leapfrog race?" Claudia called out.

Well, everyone knew how to play leapfrog. The teammates lined up and leapfrogged in turn till someone reached the finishing line.

When the Blue team won, there was an explosion. "Buddy didn't jump with both feet!" Becca screamed.

"Yes, he did!" Buddy protested.

Even Charlotte was upset. "You didn't! You cheated."

"Well, Vanessa did the same thing!" Jordan yelled.

"Liar liar, pants on fire!" Vanessa cried.

"I don't want to be in this stupid thing," Buddy said.

"Yeah," Jamie agreed. "I want to ride my bike."

"'Run for Your Money' silly-billy-goo-goo," Claire mumbled.

Claudia, Stacey, Jessi, and Mal gave each other a Look. "What about making up our own events?" Claudia suggested. "Silly stuff, like, I don't know . . ."

"Water-bomb!" Adam bellowed.

"What's *that*?" Margo asked.

"It's like a hot potato," Adam said. "Only you use a water balloon. Whoever lets it break is out."

"We've got some balloons in the kitchen cupboard!" Jamie shouted.

"Wait!" Claudia called out. "We can't do this without swimsuits!"

"*We're* wearing them already!" Adam exclaimed. "We were going to go to the pool."

"I'll get mine!" Jamie said, running inside.

"It's not fair!" Buddy complained.

"Let's go and see if we can find some raincoats inside," Jessi suggested.

"Yeah!" squealed the Barrett kids.

As they ran indoors with Jessi, the Pike kids stripped to their swimsuits.

"Stacey, can you keep an eye on Lucy for a minute?" Claudia asked.

"Of course."

Claudia raced inside and found the balloons. She filled four of them in the kitchen sink (not too full) and brought them out. Buddy and Suzi followed, dressed in plastic ponchos, with Jessi close behind.

The teams lined up and Claudia threw the first balloon in the air. Up it went, all wobbly-looking. And down it came—on Nicky's head.

Sploosh! "Owwww!"

The triplets exploded with laughter. Claudia was sure Nicky would burst into tears. But he said "Oops!" and started laughing, too.

The second balloon ended up watering the next-door neighbours' lawn. The third rolled under Charlotte's leg, where it— well, died a wet death. The fourth actually stayed in the air a long time, for at least six or seven passes.

Next came the race of the giants. Each "giant" was a little kid perched on the shoulders of a big kid, with beach towels or

45

old tablecloths wrapped around each pair so they looked like one huge person.

Jamie's big idea was the "Baby Jester" contest. Whoever made Lucy laugh the most was the winner. Lucy *loved* that—until it was Buddy's turn. His idea of jesting was a frantic dance, with a frozen grin, flailing legs, and some authentic war screams.

Lucy was horrified. The contest ended then and there.

Oh. There was one other event. Teddy bear volleyball. That finished up with little bits of white cotton stuffing all over the garden, leaving a very saggy Paddington bear.

A ruined garden. A traumatized baby. Eleven children with wet clothes. It was one of Claudia's toughest (and most fun) jobs.

Well, at least there was that frozen Milky Way to look forward to.

5th CHAPTER

I'd never heard Richard laugh so much. His face was red. When he put down the phone, he sat at the dinner table and said, "That was Jack Arnold. After seeing us this morning, the twins *insisted* he join the underwear race. So the Arnolds went out and bought some boxer shorts for him."

"Did they get those sweet heart ones?" Mum asked.

"No," Richard said. "Huge pictures of Garfield. See what we've started?"

Mary Anne put her hand over her mouth and giggled.

I laughed, too, even though the thought of Mr Arnold in Garfield boxer shorts wasn't all that hilarious to me.

I was being very, very good. I was making sure I looked happy, cheerful and pleasant. I had already ruined the morning, and I was determined not to talk about California for the rest of that Saturday.

We'd sent out for Chinese food that night, which is one of my favourite things to do. The meal was fantastic, and at the end we pulled crackers and read our fortunes.

"'You will inherit a great deal of money,'" Mum read. "Hey, great! Dinner's on me."

Richard looked up with a dry, disappointed expression. "'A handsome stranger will enter your life.'"

"'Success is one per cent inspiration and ninety-nine per cent perspiration,'" Mary Anne read. "Yuck."

I stared at my fortune. I couldn't believe what it said.

Have you ever had a psychic experience? You know, spirits and ESP and things like that? Well, I know that stuff is real—and I was getting a signal.

I cleared my throat, then read, "'You will be going on a long journey to a faraway place.'"

There was a silence. I'm sure it had lasted a split-second, but it felt like a *long* time.

"Well," Richard said finally. "Sounds . . . exotic."

"These things are so silly," I lied.

"Okay, whose turn to wash up?" Mum asked quickly.

"Mine!" I jumped up from the dinner table.

I grabbed my plate and carried it to the sink. "Thanks!" I said cheerfully to each family member who dumped a plate on the worktop. As I loaded the dishwasher, Mary Anne wandered in and began wiping down the worktops. Richard and Mum were bustling around in the dining room.

"That was so *weird*," Mary Anne whispered.

"Hm?"

But I knew what she meant. And she knew I knew. When Richard walked in carrying a pile of empty takeaway boxes, Mary Anne just gave me a Look. A "We'll talk later" Look.

When I'd finished loading the dishwasher, we ran up to my bedroom and closed the door.

It was Mary Anne who spoke first. "I suppose it's really going to happen, isn't it?"

"I thought I was the only one who believed in fortunes," I said.

Mary Anne shrugged. "Well . . . I do, too, sometimes. Logan once got one that said he would reach his most desired goal, and the next day he scored a touchdown." I looked at her blankly, and she said, "You have to go over the *goal* line to score. See?"

I plopped down on my bed. I couldn't hold it back any more. The words just gushed out. "Oh, Mary Anne, I hope it *is* true. I mean, I don't want to upset you or anything, but I feel so . . . cut off. I want to be there if my dad decides to marry Carol. I want to really spend time with Jeff. I mean, I know he can be a pain, but I love him."

I had to be careful talking about Jeff. He visited us some time ago, and it wasn't that wonderful. Jeff and Richard didn't get along, then Mary Anne got angry with Jeff, then I got angry with *her*. . . What a mess.

"It's okay," Mary Anne said gently. "I think you should go."

"Do you?"

Mary Anne nodded. "Yes. I've been thinking about it. Of course I'll miss you a lot. But if you stay, you're just going to feel sad. And seeing you like that would be terrible." She bowed her head and said softly, "Besides, six months isn't *so* long."

"Oh, Mary Anne. I promise I'll write every day—"

I stopped. What was I talking about? No one had given me permission to go. There I was, all excited, and the whole thing was just a dream.

"Anyway," I continued, "we shouldn't talk about it. What if Mum says no?"

"What about your dad?" Mary Anne asked. "Have you told him how you feel?"

"Well, no, not exactly."

"Why don't you phone him? He would have to be part of this decision, too."

"I suppose so, but . . . I don't know. If I ask *his* permission, and I haven't even got Mum's, that would be like going behind her back."

"I don't mean ask permission. Not now. Just *talk*, Dawn. Tell him how torn up you feel. You can't just keep this inside."

Leave it to Mary Anne. When it comes to emotional things, she always knows what to do.

I took a deep breath. I looked at the clock. It was 8:27, which meant 5:27 in California. Dad and Jeff would probably be at home. If I didn't phone now, I might chicken out.

"Okay." I stood up and walked to the top of the stairs. "Mum?" I called. "I'm going to use the phone!"

"Okay, darling!" she called back. I could hear the TV blaring some classical music. Probably one of Richard's beloved concerts they broadcast on TV and radio at the same time. I knew I'd be safe for at least an hour.

"Good luck," Mary Anne said, slipping away to her room.

"Thanks." I walked into Mum and

Richard's bedroom and closed the door. I still felt a bit sneaky, but I'd already made my decision.

Sitting down on the bed, I picked up the phone and tapped out my dad's number.

"He*llo*!" sang a sweet and chirpy female voice.

My stomach tied itself in a knot. It was definitely *not* the voice I'd expected.

"Carol?" I said.

"Yes! Who's speaking?"

"Er, Dawn. Dawn Schafer."

"Well, hello, Dawn *Schafer*!" Carol laughed. "Did you think I'd forgotten your last name?"

I couldn't work out why that was so funny. "No, I—"

"How *are* you? Oh, wow! This is so cool. I was just thinking about you."

Oh, wow? So cool? I had to shake my head. This was a thirty-two-year-old I was talking to. "Really? I'm fine. And you?"

"Great. I'm making an exotic salad—radicchio, edible flowers, sun-dried tomatoes. You should see it! Oh, your dad will be so happy that you've phoned! I'd better give the phone to him. Besides, I've got olive oil and lemon juice all over my fingers. When are we going to *see* you?"

"Well, I—"

"Oops, here he is! He's taking the phone out of my hand. Oops! *'Bye, Dawn!'*"

"'Bye!" I said.

(I thought I liked Carol. Maybe I was wrong.)

"Hey, how's my Sunshine?" Dad greeted me.

"Hi, Dad!" I felt all my gloominess wash away. I wish you could hear my dad's voice. It's so deep and laid-back and comforting. Honestly, I think he could have been a TV announcer. "Have you got a few minutes to talk?"

"For you? As long as you want!"

We chatted for a minute. Then, taking a deep breath, I said, "Dad, er . . . I've been thinking really hard about how much I miss California."

"Yes. But you know, darling, I think Connecticut is one of the most beautiful—"

"Well, not California, exactly, but *you*. And Jeff. And my friends. And even Mrs Bruen." (She's my dad's housekeeper.) "What I mean is, I really want to move back for a while. Like for a few months. I'm not asking *permission*. I just want to know what you think."

"What do I think? Well—I—Dawn, are you sure about this?"

Gulp. I felt as if I were in a lift that'd just dropped ten floors. Dad was supposed to sound *thrilled*—or at least a little positive.

"Yes, I'm sure," I said. I explained all my reasons, and he listened silently.

At the end, I could hear him sigh. "How does your mum feel about it?"

"Not too great."

"Mm, I didn't think so. I mean, with Jeff already out here."

"You don't sound too happy, either, Dad." I was fighting the urge to cry.

"Oh, Dawn, I'd be *overjoyed* if you came. Don't get me wrong. It's just that . . . well, I hope you're not setting yourself up for disappointment. It's not easy going back to a place after you've left."

"I know, but I don't want to *move* back. It would just be temporary."

Dad was silent for a long time. At last he said, "I suppose I should talk to your mum."

"Mum?" I was mortified. "But—she doesn't—she'll think—"

"Don't worry. I'll explain everything. I'll say you phoned only to *discuss* the idea, not to make me side with you against her. Okay?"

"Okay. I'll go and get her."

I ran out of the room. Mary Anne was peering from her doorway with huge, questioning eyes. I smiled and ran down-stairs.

Mum was practically asleep, watching some old bearded man conduct an orchestra full of younger bearded men and unbearded women. "Mum?" I said.

"Huh?"

"Dad's on the phone. Can you talk to him?"

Mum looked a little—well, annoyed, shocked, scared, wary, you name it. She picked up the extension in the kitchen. "Hello?"

I pretended I had things to do down-stairs. I walked around the living room. Then I wiped down the clean dining room table. Then I inspected the dishwasher.

I heard snatches of conversation: ". . . mid-term enrolment . . . after-school activities . . . statewide achievement standards . . . *sure* I feel that way. I'm human . . . six months . . . you think so? . . . That would be nice . . . so sad lately. . . ."

It was a *long* conversation. My imagi-nation was going wild dreaming up ways to make myself look busy. By the time Mum rang off, I was examining the front hall carpet.

I ran into the kitchen. "Well?" I said. "Did you talk about it?"

I expected Mum's face to look all grumpy

and thoughtful. But she gave me a warm smile. "Of course we did. It's the *only* thing we talked about. Give us some time, Dawn. It's a big change. We're going to sleep on it and talk again tomorrow. Okay?"

"Okay," I said. I nodded and went upstairs. I was cool. I was reasonable. I walked straight to my room. I shut the door behind me.

Then I buried my face in my pillow and screamed at the top of my lungs.

Mary Anne came running in. "Did they say yes?"

"No," I said, grinning.

"Then why are you screaming?"

"They didn't say no. And Mum wasn't angry!"

Mary Anne looked at me as if I were crazy. "Er, okay. I suppose that's progress."

"Yes," I said.

Mary Anne gave me another curious look, then went back to her homework.

Me? I was happy to have the matter out in the open. I was sure that if I stuck to my guns, I had a chance.

And all I needed was a chance.

6th
CHAPTER

"Yes, it *is* early in the school year, but I'm not sure you understand," Mum was saying into the phone.

It was Sunday afternoon. Mum and Dad were talking for the second time that day. Their earlier conversation had been horrible. Mum had been bad-tempered, and obviously Dad hadn't been any better. Luckily, they seemed to be pretty calm now.

Mary Anne was sitting for the Kuhns, and Richard was food-shopping, so I had to face the tension alone. What do I like to do to relieve tension? Talk on the phone! Makes sense, doesn't it? So instead, I decided to read a mystery—in the living room, conveniently within earshot of the kitchen.

"They're already a few weeks into the

curriculum," Mum continued. "Yes, I suppose I should ask Mrs Amer."

Whoa! This was a big breakthrough. Mrs Amer is my guidance counsellor! So Mum and Dad were no longer talking about whether I *should* go, but how I would adjust if I *did* go!

I pulled myself together. A real "yes" was still a long way off. I knew I should keep calm, calm, calm.

"Okay, what else?" Mum said. "Yes, she does date . . . occasionally. Steady? Well, no, but there is a boy she writes to pretty often."

I blushed. That boy is Logan Bruno's cousin, Lewis. We had a great time when he visited, but we're more pen pals than anything now.

"Yes," Mum continued. "She has to be home by nine on weekdays and ten at weekends, unless she's sitting late . . . *Baby*sitting. . . . Clothes? Er, yes, she chooses them herself. She's thirteen, you know."

Hmm. Dad was asking some pretty serious questions—some pretty stupid ones, too. I think he was just trying to find out all he could about my life now. Visits are one thing, but Dad was going to have to be a parent to a teenage girl.

Maybe. *Maybe.* I had to take things one step at a time.

When Mum rang off, I debated running into the kitchen. But before I could make up my mind, I heard her tapping out another number.

"Hi, Linda. It's Sharon Spier. I just need to know the current prices for plane tickets to Los Angeles . . . I haven't got a date yet. How far in advance do flights book up? . . . Uh-huh, right. . . Well, thanks a lot. . . Okay, 'bye."

Plane tickets? My jaw almost hit the floor. I flew into the kitchen. Mum was scribbling something on a pad of paper.

"Mum?" I squeaked.

She smiled knowingly. "Just checking things out. Air fares are so complicated these days."

"But those things you and Dad were talking about. . ."

"You weren't supposed to hear that!" Mum laughed. "We'll discuss it over dinner with the whole family."

"*Over dinner?* Come on, Mum. That's not fair. I'm dying to know what's happened! What did Dad say? You decided something, didn't you? Otherwise you wouldn't want to talk about it to the whole family! Right? Oh, please please please tell me."

Mum kept smiling, although I thought I could see tears in her eyes. "Okay. Sit down, darling, before you fly through the window."

I sat.

"We just don't know whether or not the Palo City school is teaching the same things as SMS," she began. "If not, you could end up terribly bored *or* terribly lost. Now, I need to talk to Mrs Amer tomorrow, and your dad's going to talk to a guidance counsellor out there—"

"And if they say it's all right?" I butted in.

"Well, *if* they convince us that you'll be able to cope with the change, then yes, we'll let you go for six months."

I rocketed out of my chair and threw my arms around her. "Oh! You are the *best*, wonderfullest, understandingest mum in the universe!"

"Darling, please don't get your hopes up yet," Mum said gently. "Let's wait to hear what your counsellor says."

"Right." I nodded and stood up. "I understand."

Ding-dong! "Delivery man!"

It was Richard. He pushed open the front door and clomped through the living room, loaded down with four huge shopping bags.

I've no idea how he managed to ring the doorbell.

Mum and I ran out and helped bring in the other bags. They completely filled the kitchen worktop.

"Quite a haul, huh?" Richard said proudly.

Richard goes shopping with a boxful of money-off coupons organized by category. He takes his calculator and makes sure only to buy groceries that are on special offer. Then he works out the percentage he's saved on the usual prices.

Mum and I looked in the bags. "Did you remember the marrow?" Mum asked.

Richard's smile disappeared. A mistake! I don't know who was more surprised, Richard or Mum and me.

Well, we managed to reassure Richard that he'd done a great job shopping. And he did bring us some slices of fabulous prepared lasagne for dinner (vegetarian for me).

While we were eating, Mum broke the news to Mary Anne and Richard about her conversation with Dad. The four of us talked about it then, but only a bit. No one wanted to talk about it *too* much until the trip was definite.

Later on Mary Anne and I squirrelled

away in my room. "I'm *so* nervous!" Mary Anne squeaked.

"*You're* nervous?" I said. "How do you think *I* feel? What if Dad phones tomorrow and says the kids out there are studying Ancient Streptococcus or something?"

Mary Anne burst out laughing. "Ancient Streptococcus? What's that?"

"I don't know. I made it up." I began pacing up and down. "Oh, I can't stand this. How am I going to sleep? And what about tomorrow at school? What am I going to tell everybody?"

"Nothing," Mary Anne replied. "There's nothing definite to tell."

"But Kristy's going to want to know straight away. Remember when I went to visit Jeff when he was ill? That was only for a couple of *weeks*, and it was hard to replace me!"

I realized how conceited that sounded, but Mary Anne understood what I meant.

"But suppose your parents say no, Dawn? Not that I'm wishing that, but just suppose? Then you'll upset everybody for no reason."

I sighed. Mary Anne was right. It was best to keep it quiet.

I was a wreck the next day. Every time I walked past the guidance office I could have sworn they were talking about me. I've no idea what happened in any of my classes—except that during maths Alan Gray (the Official SMS Jerk) kept cupping his hands over his mouth and saying, "Come in, Dawn. This is Earth. Do you read me?" At lunch I managed to dip my hair in a glass of tomato juice (*very* cool). Claudia helped me clean it off in the girls' toilets—and I practically exploded from wanting to tell her my secret.

After the last bell, I met Mary Anne in front of school and we *ran* home. Mum was at work, so I threw my books on the kitchen floor and rang her office.

"Good afternoon, Mrs Ballmer speaking."

"Hi! May I speak to Mrs Schafer?" I blurted.

"Who?"

"Mrs . . . Mrs Spier?"

"No, this is Mrs *Ballmer*. B-A-L-L—"

"Sharon! Is Sharon Spier there, please?"

"Oh. Er, just a moment."

I was dying. My stomach felt like a pretzel. I hoped Mrs Ballmer wouldn't go wandering away and forget about the phone.

"Hello, Sharon Spier here."

"Mum, it's me! Hi! Did you phone Mrs Amer?"

"I certainly did—"

"And did you phone Dad?"

"Yes, and—"

"Did he phone the counsellor there?"

"Yes, Dawn—"

"Well, what did they say?"

Mum laughed. "Let me finish a sentence. A couple of the courses you're taking now have a slightly different emphasis in the SMS curriculum."

"You mean they're harder?"

"Well, some harder, some easier, it seems. But the point is, both counsellors think you shouldn't have any trouble making up the work—either moving there or moving back here."

"Really?"

"Really."

"So that means I can go?"

"Yes, it does. I've booked you a flight for three weeks from last Saturday."

"*AAAAAAAAAAAARRRGGHHHHHHH!*" I screamed. "Ooh, sorry!"

"That's okay," Mum said. "I've got another ear."

"Oh, Mum, thank you! Thank you! I love you so much. You're the greatest."

"All I can say is, you'd better write."

"Every day! Twice a day!"

"Well, I'd even accept once a week. Now

listen, darling, I've got to get back to work. We'll celebrate tonight, okay?"

"Okay. 'Bye!"

"'Bye."

I slammed the phone down. Mary Anne was standing two centimetres away from me, grinning like crazy. We threw our arms around each other and *shrieked*.

"I knew it!" Mary Anne said. "Tell me everything."

I repeated what my mum had told me. Mary Anne nodded excitedly.

"What a relief!" I said. "Now I can feel human again. I couldn't stand not talking about this!"

"What about the meeting today?" Mary Anne asked. "Are you going to break the news?"

"I suppose so. Do you think I should?"

"Why not?"

"Maybe I should phone Claudia in advance so she can hide a cake in her sock drawer or something."

Mary Anne giggled. "Dawn, I'm so happy for you! You're like your old self again."

"California, here I come!" I screamed.

Whoa! Calm down, Dawn, I told myself. I realized I was being totally inconsiderate of Mary Anne's feelings. As if I were happy to be leaving her.

But she just smiled and kept asking me questions about my trip. No tears. Not even a sniffle. She seemed just as happy as I was.

For a moment, just a moment, I wondered whether Mary Anne was really going to miss me.

But I pushed that thought out of my mind. I couldn't wait to tell my friends the news.

7th CHAPTER

"This meeting will come to order!" Kristy barked.

I had sat in Claud's room for five whole minutes without saying a word. I wanted to wait for the perfect moment to break my news.

"Has anyone got any club business?" Kristy asked.

That was it.

"I do!" I called out. "I'm going to be moving back to California for six months!"

Cheers rang out. A brass band clanged through the room. Reporters gathered in a circle around me.

Well, not exactly. My friends stared at me blankly, as if I'd made my announcement in Swedish.

At last Stacey asked, "Really?"

I nodded.

"Is this some sort of emergency?" Mallory asked.

"No," I said. Patiently I told my story. I made sure to mention (several times) how much I would miss everybody, and how I would definitely come back when the six months were over.

At last Stacey looked at me with a warm smile. "Dawn, you sound so happy," she said.

"But *six months?*" Claudia chimed in. "We're going to miss you so much!"

"Yes!" Jessi, Mal and Stacey agreed.

Then everyone began talking at once:

"What are you taking?"

"Is it still swimming weather there?"

"Are you going to have to go to school?" (That was Claudia's question.)

"Send pictures!"

"Send pictures of guys on the beach!"

"Just send the guys!"

Before long we were all giggling. All except Kristy. She was *trying* not to look angry, but she couldn't keep the frown from her face.

"Ahem!" Kristy said at last. "Shouldn't we talk about the consequences of this?"

Claudia rolled her eyes. "Come on, Kristy. She's not *moving*. She's just going on a visit."

"Right," Kristy replied. "And we'll be

one member short for six months. That's twenty-six weeks, times three meetings a week is . . . what, Stacey?"

"Er, seventy-eight," Stacey answered. "But Kristy—"

"Seventy-eight meetings is a lot," Kristy said. "As it is, the seven of us are booked solid. In case you haven't noticed, we've been calling on Logan and Shannon all the time. What's going to happen when we *lose* one member?"

"Kristy, come on—" Claudia began.

"Well, we've got to think of these things, right?" Kristy protested. "I mean, I know you miss your dad, Dawn. But six months just seems like a lot."

To tell you the truth, I did feel awful about leaving the club. But I didn't expect Kristy to react that way.

"Kristy," I said, "I'm not doing this to hurt you lot. I wouldn't dream of it. I tried to explain. I *have* to go. It's the most important thing in my life right now."

"Hey, don't worry," Claudia reassured me. "We'll work out what to do."

Kristy just glared at her.

"Look," I said quickly. "I have thought about this. I know you'll have to replace me temporarily, and I promise I'll help solve the problem before I leave. It's the least I can do."

RINNNNGG!

The sound of the phone was such a relief.

"Hello?" Claudia said, snatching the receiver. "Oh, hi, Mrs Hobart . . . Okay, I'll call back in a minute."

She hung up and said to Mary Anne, "A week from Wednesday? Everyone wants a sitter for that day."

Mary Anne nodded. "Parent-teacher meetings at SES." (That's Stoneybrook Elementary School.) She looked up from the BSC record book and said, "Well, we're all busy, but I'm sure Logan wouldn't mind. He loves the Hobart kids. I'll phone him if you want."

"I'm sure you will," Claudia said with a sly smile.

"Maybe he'd want to be my replacement while I'm away," I added.

"Logan definitely prefers being an associate," Kristy said. "Besides, remember when we did ask him to be a permanent member? It didn't work out very well."

Kristy was right. Once I'd gone to California for a few weeks when Jeff was ill and Logan had become a regular member. But apparently Logan's football teammates had made his life horrible with teasing and practical jokes.

"Besides," Kristy added, "if Logan or

Shannon became a regular member, then we'd be short of an associate member."

"Well, it's better than nothing," I said.

Mary Anne had already got through to Logan on the phone. She explained the situation to him, mentioned the Hobart job, and asked if he would replace me. Then her face became very solemn. "Mm-hm . . . I know ʼ . . . it must be . . . well, that would help. . . . Uh-huh, I'll tell them. 'Bye."

She rang off and turned to Kristy. "He says he'll sit for the Hobarts, but football practice is getting really intense now, so he couldn't be a full-time member."

Oh, well. One down. "I'll phone Shannon," I said.

She was at home, too. I filled her in and asked her the big question.

"I wish I could," was her response. "But I'm starting this after-school tutoring project for the honour society. It's going to last at least two months. But maybe afterwards . . ."

Two down.

Kristy wasn't too jolly about the news. "I don't want you to feel guilty, Dawn," she said, "but this is going to be a big mess."

"I'm not sure about that," Mary Anne spoke up. "I mean, how often is *every single one* of us busy?"

"A week from Wednesday," Kristy quickly replied.

"*Kristy!*" Stacey joined in. "That's really unusual. We hardly ever have to turn away work. I think we'll be able to survive without a seventh full-time member for a while."

I could tell everyone was avoiding the obvious possibility. So I brought it up. "What about taking on a new member?" I asked.

"You mean temporarily, while you're away?" Jessi asked.

"Well . . . yes," I said.

"Not to *replace* you," Mary Anne added. "We'd never do that."

She glanced at Kristy, but Kristy only said, "It's not easy getting new members."

"Dawn was a new member once," Claudia pointed out brightly.

"So were Janet and Leslie," Kristy replied. (Those were two members who didn't work out well, back before I joined the BSC.) "Besides, what do we do with the new person after six months? Kick her out?"

"Look," Stacey said, "we don't have to solve this problem right now. Dawn's not leaving for three weeks. Let's enjoy her while she's here."

"Oh!" Claudia blurted. "I think I've got

some popcorn rice cakes." She hopped off her bed and started rummaging around in her chest of drawers.

Kristy sighed. "I'm sorry. It's just that we're getting very busy."

As if to prove Kristy's point, the phone began ringing—and it hardly stopped until six o'clock. In between we talked about a few other things, like "Run for Your Money" preparations and Jessi's forthcoming trip to Oakley.

But the atmosphere remained pretty tense. It was hard not to think about my decision and how it affected everybody. Leaving Stoneybrook was getting more complicated than I expected.

8th CHAPTER

Saturday

If you've never been to a big Greek party, you should go. Whoa. You wouldn't believe it. The Papadakises were having a family reunion, and what a family! I mean, Zeus didn't come down with his thunderbolts or anything, but he didn't really need to. The kids provided plenty of fireworks...

Five days had passed since I'd mentioned my trip in the BSC meeting. Kristy was no longer quite so snarly. In fact, she apologized to me and wished me luck.

Now that my trip was a reality, I'd started to pack. Well, sort of. I'd opened up a couple of suitcases on my floor and thrown a few clothes in.

The truth? Somehow now I wasn't as excited as I had been. I suppose the reality of my trip was sinking in. My head was spinning with questions. Was it selfish to abandon the BSC—and Mum and Mary Anne and Richard—for six months? Why was everyone actually so *upbeat* about my decision lately? Were they secretly glad I was going? What if I hated living in California?

Anyway, while I was pondering these questions, Kristy was helping the Papadakises on the day of their reunion. Mr Papadakis's two sisters were coming from New York with *their* families. Also coming were a lot of other cousins and aunts and uncles and friends Kristy had never heard of.

Kristy arrived at their house early, to look after the kids while the Papadakises got organized for the party. The Papadakises have got a huge garden. There's a basketball court in the drive and a badminton area by the garage. On this day, behind the house were dozens of card tables, covered with paper tablecloths and disposable place settings. In the air was a pungent, mouth-watering barbecue smell. Mr Papadakis was putting a tape deck and loudspeakers on the back porch. Kristy approached him to say hello, but something made her stop in her tracks.

Off to the right, at the edge of the woods behind the Papadakises' house, were four barbecue pits in the ground. Above each one was an animal carcass on a rotating spit.

I'm so glad I wasn't there. I think I would have thrown up. Kristy, who isn't upset by much, felt rather queasy, too.

"Delicious, huh?" Mr Papadakis called out. "Those are lambs, fresh from the farm! You have never tasted anything so tender. Here, let me cut you some before the guests arrive."

"*No!*" Kristy said, almost shouting. "I mean, maybe later. I had a late breakfast."

"I'll save you some pieces," Mr Papadakis insisted.

"Hi, Kristy!"

Hannie and Linny came running out of the house. (Hannie's seven and Linny's nine.) They were followed by two-year-old

Sari, who toddled out with a little moon-face smile. "Kiss-tee!" she squealed.

"Hello!" Mrs Papadakis chimed in, backing through the door with the two tinfoil-covered trays. She put them down on a picnic table and smiled at Kristy. "Our special *spanakopita* and *tiropita*. Want to sneak a piece?"

"Thanks, but I think I'll go and play with the kids," Kristy said. She didn't know *what* would be peeping out at her from under that foil.

Before long Kristy was really working. Linny fell and cut his knee. Hannie dropped a glass when she went into the kitchen. Sari kept wanting to play near the barbecue pits.

When the guests started to arrive, Mr Papadakis turned on the tape deck. This loud, exotic music blared out, with a strong beat and a guitarlike instrument, which Mr Papadakis called a *bouzouki*. (Kristy liked the bouzouki but thought the singers sounded as if they had indigestion.)

Well, the Papadakis family turned out to be absolutely huge. Kristy counted five Nikos, four Alexandras, three Peters, two Marias, two Takis and a Gus. Luckily a lot of them were too old to need sitters (including fifteen-year-old Niko who was extremely cute, according to Kristy).

So you can imagine Kristy's surprise when some of the neighbourhood kids decided to wander over.

"Linny! Hannie! Hi!" Bill Korman yelled.

He and his sister Melody ran into the garden, all wide-eyed. (Bill's nine and Melody's seven.)

"Er, listen, you lot," Kristy said. "I don't know if Hannie and Linnie have got permission—"

"Hey! Welcome to the party!" Mr Papadakis's voice boomed out. He trotted over to Bill and Melody and said, "Are you hungry? Would you like to try some lamb?"

Melody made a face. "Have you got any Pringles?"

"Melody!" Bill scolded. "Be polite."

"Pringles coming right up!" Mr Papadakis said, running into the house.

When he got back, with Pringles *and* Wheat Thins *and* Ritz Crackers, Kristy's brother and step-siblings appeared.

"Karen! Andrew! David Michael! Good to see you!" Mr Papadakis said.

"Yum! Ritz Crackers!" Andrew answered. (He's four; Karen and David Michael are seven.)

"Sit and enjoy," Mr Papadakis went on, putting the packets on one of the card tables. The kids gathered around like flies around honey.

Eight charges. For any other babysitter, that would be a lot. For Kristy, it was an opportunity.

She was looking around, trying to work out how she could organize a soccer game, when Linny said, "Hey, Kristy! Can we practise for 'Run for Your Money'?"

Perfect. Even though I'm sure Kristy would have thought of it herself (hrrmph). "Of course!" she said. "What shall we start with?"

"Basketball shooting!" the Korman kids screamed.

"Bang bang!" Sari said.

Linny ran into the garage and got two basketballs. "I shoot first!" he bellowed.

"No way!" David Michael protested. "We're guests!"

"Let's make teams," Kristy suggested. "How about the Papadakises and Andrew against the Kormans and Karen and David Michael—"

"We'll thrash 'em," Linny said.

Bill stuck out his chest. "No, you won't!"

"Beanpole!" Linny said.

"Nit head!"

While they were arguing, a couple of the older cousins grabbed the basketballs and started playing.

After lots of crying and some general pandemonium, Kristy explained "Run for Your Money" to everyone. Well, the Papadakis cousins loved the idea. The trouble was, they didn't live in Stoneybrook *or* Lawrenceville. But that didn't stop them. After basketball, the kids held a massive three-legged race that ended up almost toppling the food table over. Sari wanted to join in, so Kristy tied her leg to a Cabbage Patch doll's leg.

Out came the cameras. I think Sari will be haunted by pictures of that event for the rest of her life.

Next, Kristy set up a game of horseshoes for the kids. Of course, Linny wanted to have the first turn.

He lifted a horseshoe and began spinning his arm around. "The windup . . ."

"Linny," Kristy warned, "this isn't baseball!"

"And . . . the . . ."

"Linny!" Kristy tried again.

". . . Pitch!" Linny let go of the horseshoe too late—far too late. The horseshoe went flying towards the house.

"Heads up!" Kristy shouted.

Everyone looked around in confusion. The horseshoe came hurtling down.

Plop! It landed in a plateful of gooey pastries.

"Oooops!" Linny muttered.

A roar of laughter went up. "Hey, it's good luck!" one of the aunts called out.

After a couple more events, it was time for Sari's nap. Then Kristy and the kids ate some food (by the way, she said the lamb *was* delicious, but that's a carnivore for you). After that came dessert and some Greek dancing to wild music. The guests joined hands and snaked around the garden.

By the time the party was over, Kristy was exhausted (yes, Kristy). She said goodbye to the Papadakises and walked home with David Michael, Karen and Andrew.

I found out *much* later what they talked about after the party—me!

"Kristy!" Karen said. "Are you sad about Dawn?"

Kristy nodded (at least she *said* she did). "Yes. I'm going to miss her."

"You know what we did when Amanda Delaney moved away?" Karen asked. "I gave her a party. You should do that for Dawn. It was really fun."

"Yeah!" Andrew and David Michael said.

Kristy's eyebrows rose. "Hmmmm. Not a bad idea."

She ran to the phone. First she rang Mary Anne, then Mallory, then Claudia, then Stacey. She nearly rang Jessi, until she realized Jessi was in Oakley for the weekend.

Everyone agreed. The party was a great idea.

And poor little old me didn't know a thing about it.

9th
CHAPTER

"Are you sure nothing's wrong?" Kristy said to Jessi.

"*Yes*," Jessi replied. "You've asked me that a million times."

Jessi was exaggerating. Our Monday meeting was only about five minutes old. But she'd spent those five minutes under her own little storm cloud. She was sitting on Claudia's floor, staring out of the window, her knees drawn up to her chin.

We'd already paid our weekly subs and taken a phone call. Claud was busy distributing goodies.

"Claudia, these are absolutely disgusting," Stacey suddenly said, holding up a plastic bag of biscuits.

"Yeah?" Claudia took the bag and read it. "'Chock Full of Chakra Macrobiotic Dessert Snacks . . . active ingredients:

comfrey leaves and kelp, sweetened with barley malt and raisin juice.'"

"Ugh!" Mallory said.

"What's kelp?" Mary Anne asked.

"Tiny green fish that swim through your bloodstream and eat bacteria," Kristy replied with a straight face.

"Really?" Claudia looked horrified.

Stacey groaned. "Don't listen to her."

Kristy just grinned.

I had to admit, even to a health food freak like me, those biscuits tasted pretty horrible.

Yes, I ate one. In fact, we actually passed them around for a tasting. Have you ever seen anyone turn green? Mary Anne did. Mal refused even to look at them. Claudia scraped off a teeny layer of one with her teeth, and brave Kristy gobbled a whole one down. Then they both devoured a box of chocolate-covered raisins to get rid of the taste.

When the bag was passed to Jessi, she didn't notice it at first. She was still staring out of the window.

"Here," Kristy said. "Your turn."

Jessi shook her head and waved the bag away.

"Hey, what's the matter?" Kristy said. "You've been grumpy since you got here."

Jessi made a face and frowned.

Luckily, Mary Anne decided to use

a little more tact. "Jessi, how was your trip?"

Jessi sighed. In a mumbly voice, still looking out of the window, she said, "Pretty terrible."

"Uh-oh!" Claudia said. "What happened?"

At last Jessi opened up. "Well, I get there, right? And Keisha's got this new haircut and is wearing make-up. We say hello and everybody goes inside for lunch. Then the bell rings and it's this new friend of hers named Jennifer, who's wearing so much perfume I can't breathe. Jennifer says, 'Is she going dressed like *that*?' Meaning me. It turns out they go to the mall every Saturday to hang around, all dressed up."

"And your aunt and uncle let her go, even though she had a visitor?" Stacey asked.

"No," Jessi replied. "They told her she couldn't go, and Jennifer made this face, like they were being so horrible. And Keisha got really upset. She and Jennifer whispered together out on the porch for half an hour while I just sat around. At last my aunt told Keisha to say goodbye and come back in—and then Keisha wouldn't even talk to anyone for the rest of the afternoon."

"You're kidding!" Mary Anne said. "How rude."

"Well, as she was being so weird, *I* asked if I could walk over to my old ballet school. I invited Keisha to go, but she said no. Anyway, it turns out my teacher divorced her husband and moved to Ohio to go to law school or something. The school's now an aerobics centre, and the new teacher wouldn't even let me in the door. So *then* I walked past my old house—and they were chopping down these two beautiful maple trees at the front. Those were *my* trees! I used to go to sleep on summer nights listening to the leaves rustling outside my bedroom window. Some guy with a chain-saw said the trees were blocking the power lines. So I went back to Keisha's, all upset—and she was angry with me because *I* went out and had such a fabulous time."

"Ugh! What a nightmare," Mal said.

"How about Sunday?" Claudia asked.

"After church we had a big roast chicken, and the Raymonds came over. They're old friends of my family."

"Well, *that* sounds nice," Mary Anne said.

"Except for the fact that Neil Raymond, their son, who used to be rather dorky and shy, is now sixteen and gorgeous. Well, he kept talking about himself the whole time—like how many touchdowns he was scoring, which vitamins he took, the best kind of white socks to wear. *Boring!* And of course, Keisha acted as if he was just fascinating. Afterwards we joked about him and Keisha seemed a bit friendlier. But by that time we had to leave."

"You need some special TLC," Claudia said. She reached under her bed and pulled out another box. "How about a Hula Hoop?"

Jessi laughed and took one. "Okay. They look better than those other things you were handing round."

"You know, going back to your old town can be strange," Stacey said. "Everything changes. The last time I went to New York, it didn't even feel like my neighbourhood. My favourite restaurant had become an ugly clothes shop, and this old cinema was being torn down to make way for a block of flats."

"Not to mention Laine," Claudia said.

"Right!" Stacey replied. "You can't even count on your old friends."

Laine had been Stacey's best friend in New York. But after Stacey moved to Stoneybrook, Laine changed. She became really snobby and cold.

Listening to Jessi and Stacey made my heart sink. What was going to happen to me? What about *my* friends and *my* neighbourhood? At least Jessi and Stacey only went on short visits, so they could leave when the going got tough.

I had made a stupid mistake, I just knew it. I was going to be like ET, the extra-terrestrial, when I returned to California. No one would know what to make of me. No one would want to be friends with a girl who planned to leave in six months!

Before long, *I* was the one looking gloomily out of the window. Kristy had launched into this huge description of her Saturday at the Papadakises', and everybody else was laughing. In my mind I saw a split-screen image. On the left side, the BSC members (minus me) were building a snowman on a crisp wintry day, throwing snowballs and sipping thermoses of hot chocolate. On the right, I was sitting in traffic on the Santa Ana Freeway in California, listening to holiday music on the car radio and looking through smog at the red-and-green cellophane wreaths hanging on the street lights.

Whoa, Dawn! Calm down! I told myself.

I tried to pay attention to the meeting. Kristy was now talking about "Run for Your Money", which was only five days away.

"We're actually going to make up two teams," she was saying. "Watson, me, Karen, Charlie and Emily Michelle—and

Mum, David Michael, Sam, Andrew and Nannie. Unless Emily Michelle insists on being in Nannie's team."

"We're making up two teams, too," Mal said, "but the triplets want to take part in every single event."

"I'm trying to get my family interested in the pie-eating contest," Claudia said. "But Janine's found out there's going to be a team trivia-quiz event, so I'll probably smile stupidly while Janine and my parents answer all the questions."

"We're going to enter Squirt for the baby race," Jessi piped up. "I want the rest of us to do the triathlon, which is a short race, a couple of low hurdles and a long jump."

An idea suddenly came to me. I couldn't believe no one had thought of it yet. "Hey, what about us?" I said.

"Huh?" Claudia replied.

"A Babysitters Club team," I explained. "You can be in more than one team, can't you? So each of us can be in a family team *and* a BSC team! We don't have to be in a lot of events, just one or two."

"That's a pretty good idea," Kristy admitted.

"Yes!" a couple of the others said.

"Hey, there's a revised list of events in the *Stoneybrook News* today." Claudia grabbed a newspaper from the mess beside her bed. "Let's decide what to enter."

We pored over the listing. People had been phoning in with suggestions, so all kinds of new contests had been added. (One was "water balloon hot potato", thanks to the triplets, I bet.)

"Limbo dancing?" Claudia said.

"Er, next suggestion," Stacey replied.

"Pet races!" Mallory exclaimed.

"I don't think we qualify," Jessi said.

At last we narrowed it down to the dance relay race (you pass a baton like in a relay race, but instead of running you dance), and an event called Mondo Ball (each team has to try to manoeuvre this gigantic ball from one side of the field to the other).

By the end of the meeting, I was feeling much better. I was even looking forward to my trip again.

I decided to phone my dad that evening. He was just as happy and friendly as ever—and incredibly excited about my visit. Jeff was practically bursting with plans for us.

You know what? I didn't care about what might have changed in California. My real reason for going out there was to see Dad and Jeff.

And *they* hadn't changed a bit.

10th CHAPTER

Thursday

Today I sat for the
Pike kids with Mallory.
It was a pretty normal
day. We played in the
yard. Nothing much
else to say.

Now, do you believe a word of that?

Mary Anne's very clever, but she doesn't know how to lie. At least she could have written something a bit more creative.

The truth was, she and Mal did a *lot* with the kids. But she didn't want to mention what, because it was a secret.

Mum drove her to the Pikes', which seemed rather odd to me, as they live just down the road. Mum insisted she had to go to the supermarket, and she was dropping Mary Anne off on the way.

Uh-huh.

Well, she went to the supermarket, all right—but *with* Mary Anne. To buy ingredients for my surprise farewell party, which was to be held on Sunday, the day after "Run for Your Money"!

(Luckily, I didn't find out about this until the party. I *love* surprises!)

The Pike kids spilled out of the house when Mary Anne and Mum arrived.

"I'll take in the bag with the chocolate chips!" Nicky yelled.

"What makes you think we've bought chocolate chips?" Mary Anne asked.

"Didn't you?" Adam said, wide-eyed.

"Dawn eats only health food," Mary Anne said. "So we're making a broccoli soufflé and preparing raw vegetables with dip."

The kids stared at her in shock. Mary Anne grinned and said, "Gotcha!"

"Let me see!" Byron cried. He grabbed a grocery bag right out of her hand.

"Careful—" Mary Anne warned.

Rrrrrip! Out came chocolate chips, devils' food cake mix, crisps, pretzels and a frozen tofu-rhubarb pie.

Can you guess which one of those items was left on the pavement by the kids?

Anyway, Mary Anne and Mum brought the rest of the stuff in. Mrs Pike ran downstairs, gave the sitters some last-minute instructions, and left with Mum.

The kitchen was instant chaos. Claire had pulled up a chair so she could help at the worktop. Nicky was trying to pull it out from underneath her. Adam was bopping Vanessa on the head with a wire egg whisk. Margo had managed to open the bag of flour and was making herself a white beard and moustache.

Phweeeeeet!

Mary Anne jumped. The kids shut up.

Mallory was standing by the sink, a huge silver whistle in her mouth. Her face lit up. "Hey, this thing really works!"

"Where did you get that?" Adam asked.

"Dad bought it," Mal replied. "He thought we might need it for 'Run for Your Money'."

"Let me try!" Jordan cried.

Mal should have tied the whistle round her neck. Before she could pull it away, Jordan grabbed it and started blowing.

"Me too!" six other voices called.

Mary Anne said she was almost deafened. Finally Mallory managed to grab the whistle away from Margo.

"Hey, what about me?" Claire complained.

"This was a mistake," Mal said.

"*Waaaaaaahh!*" Claire replied, falling to the floor.

"Baby!" Nicky taunted.

"*I'm not a babyyyyyy!*" Claire cried.

"All right!" Mal held out the whistle. "One blow—and in the living room!"

Claire ran off and actually obeyed.

When she got back, preparations for a cake had already begun. (Actually, the tofu-rhubarb pie was for me. Most of the rest of the baking was for the invited guests—which included everyone in the BSC, their siblings, and a lot of other sitting charges.)

"Can I crack the eggs? Can I?" Margo asked, grabbing an egg.

Splat.

It did crack. On the floor.

"Oops!" Margo said sheepishly.

"That's okay," Mal said. "You know how to clean it up."

Sllllosh! "Whoa!" Byron went sliding across the floor on the egg.

"Byron!" Mal moaned.

"Gross!" Adam yelled. "Let me try!"

"No!" said Mary Anne and Mal together.

As the first big clean-up of the day began, Vanessa danced around the room, composing a farewell poem aloud: "Dawn, Dawn, please don't go; we all love you so. . ." When the floor was eggless, Mary Anne patiently helped Claire measure out sugar—while Adam kept licking his fingers and sticking them in the bag. Jordan and Byron played catch with the bag of chocolate chips, keeping it from Nicky.

And soon . . . there were visitors!

Stacey and Kristy had arrived with their charges. (Stace was sitting for Charlotte Johanssen and Kristy was sitting for the Barrett kids.) Mr and Mrs Pike had agreed to let them come over to help.

"I want to help with the cake!" Buddy Barrett insisted.

"I want to play!" shouted his sister Suzi.

"Oooh, you're making chocolate chip cookies!" Charlotte cried when she saw the game of catch.

"Give it to me!" Nicky screamed.

"Whoa . . . *Whoa! Listen!*" Kristy put two fingers in her mouth and whistled.

It made Mal's metal whistle sound dainty. All noise instantly stopped. (Leave it to Kristy.)

"Okay, we've got to organize things," Kristy said. "We need a decorations committee, a baking committee and a planning committee for games."

The kids all began shouting at once. In no time, the kitchen crew had shrunk to Margo, Nicky, Claire and Buddy. Adam, Jordan and Char agreed to plan the games; and Byron, Vanessa and Suzi became the decoration team (with the "help" of little Marnie Barrett).

Of course, things didn't go perfectly. Byron almost fainted blowing up the balloons. Marnie sellotaped her fingers together and spilled glue on the carpet. Buddy dropped a garlic bulb in the cake mix (unpeeled, thank goodness). The games committee argued over everything (Adam kept suggesting sports-type things, Jordan wanted only video games, and Charlotte insisted on quiet activities like Scrabble and Twister). Vanessa disappeared into her bedroom and wasn't heard from for about an hour.

Finally at about one o'clock everybody took a break. "All hands outside for playtime!" Kristy announced.

"Yeaaaa!" the kids shouted. Everybody ran out of the back door (except for the food handlers, who had quite a bit of washing up to do first).

Mary Anne ran upstairs to get Vanessa. She found her curled up on her bed, sniffling quietly, her eyes watery. A pad of paper and a pencil were lying next to her.

"What's wrong?" Mary Anne asked, sitting down.

"N-n-nothing," Vanessa said.

Out of the corner of her eye, Mary Anne glanced at the pad of paper. On it was a huge farewell poem to me.

"Are you sad about Dawn leaving?" Mary Anne asked.

Vanessa nodded.

"Yes, I'm going to miss her, too."

"She's your *sister*," Vanessa said sympathetically.

"I know. May I read it?"

"Uh-huh."

Well, you know Mary Anne. The waterworks began right away.

"Mary Anne, are you okay?" Vanessa asked.

Mary Anne wiped her eyes. "It's *beautiful*. Would you mind if I read it to the others?"

"Do you like it?"

"I love it."

Vanessa grinned. "Okay!"

They went out to the garden. Somehow the four babysitters managed to gather the kids around the picnic table. Mallory was elected to read the poem (Mary Anne wasn't sure she'd make it through dry-eyed).

The poem went like this:

Dawn, Dawn, please don't go,
We all love you so.
Your nice to us, you make us smile
We love your hair, your laugh, your stile.
When you're away in California
We'll be so sad. we'll really ~~morn~~ moarn ya.

"That doesn't rhyme," Adam volunteered.

"She's not *dying*," Jordan remarked.

"Shhhhh!" Kristy said.

Mallory continued:

We wish you luck, tho you upset us
Please, please, please, Dawn, don't forget us.

"Too many pleases," Adam murmured.

But his comment faded into the air. All the kids were looking sad. Mary Anne was dabbing her eyes.

Sigh. I've got wonderful friends, haven't I?

11th CHAPTER

"On your marks . . . get set . . . go!"

I was running, carrying a suitcase in each hand and a rucksack on my back.

My feet weren't even touching the ground. I passed Richard, Mum and every member of the BSC except Mary Anne, who was ahead of me. But I couldn't see the finishing line anywhere. When I caught up with Mary Anne, she smiled at me. "Okay," she said. "You can stop now. . . Dawn? *Dawn?*"

I couldn't stop. I was flying. Signs whizzed past me: *Ohio, Minnesota, Nebraska, Utah.* At last I made out a huge sign that said WELCOME TO PALO CITY. Dad and Jeff were next to it, but they didn't see me. "Dad!" I screamed.

"Dawn?" Mary Anne said.

My eyes snapped open. "Huh?"

100

Mary Anne was leaning over my bed. "Are you okay? You were really tossing and turning."

"Yes, it was just a dream," I mumbled.

"Well, hurry and come downstairs. We're having a power breakfast!" With a big smile, Mary Anne left.

I sat up and let the dream fade from my mind. Time for a reality check. I was in my room, and it was Saturday, the day of "Run for Your Money". I glanced out of my window. Clouds were whipping by, but the weather didn't look too bad.

Suddenly I was in the real world. This was going to be a big day, and I was so excited!

I put on my one-piece swimsuit, then threw a tracksuit over it, and jammed my feet into a pair of trainers. As I ran downstairs, the smell of pancakes and eggs and bacon hit me.

I could do without the pig part, but I *love* pancakes and I was even in the mood for eggs.

Mum was racing around the kitchen, dressed in very chic running shorts, with a matching top, leg warmers and brand-new white trainers. Richard was wearing a baggy, stiff pair of jeans; a paint-stained sweat-shirt; and his brown, hideous "comfortable walking shoes". Mary Anne was busily pouring orange juice and laying the table.

"Power up!" Richard called out, flipping pancakes on to a plate.

"The breakfast of champions!" Mum said, making a muscle with her left arm. She was cutting green peppers into these huge, unusual shapes.

"Can I help?" I asked.

"Of course," Mum said. "I was making you a vegetarian omelette."

"Thanks," I said. "I'll take over if you want."

No protest from Mum. Now, I love her and she's got a lot of talents. Unfortunately, cooking isn't one of them. I made sure to cut the peppers into sizes that wouldn't choke me, then went to work on the mushrooms.

Before long we were sitting down to the most enormous breakfast I've ever eaten. We chomped away like crazy, especially Richard. "I got up early for calisthenics and a jog," he boasted.

"Three press-ups and half-way round the block," Mum said.

"Well, it's been a while," Richard replied.

We gobbled down almost all the food and hurried outside. Mary Anne brought along a hat with a visor and three different bottles of sunblock (her skin's extremely sensitive to the sun). "Gentlemen, start your engine!" Richard called out as he turned the key in the ignition.

"Dad, you're so goofy today," Mary Anne said.

"Gorsh!" Richard replied in a Goofy voice.

We sped to the high school, laughing all the way. Even before we arrived, we could feel the excitement. Three blocks away, cars were bumper-to-bumper, honking horns. Kids were leaning out of windows, cheering and waving banners. We ended up parking about a block away.

Well, you should have seen the high school playing field. It was *jammed*. Things had been piled along the sidelines—sacks, boxes of bandannas for three-legged races, ropes for tug-of-war, hoses, balloons, buckets, balls, inflatable paddles. A huge blob (which I assumed was the Mondo Ball) was resting against the stands. Other stuff was still being piled on. On one side of the field were stalls, and a couple of rides for kids (a Ferris wheel and rotating space-ships). The sideshow games—pinball and video machines, hoopla, archery—were on the other side. Balloons and pennants waved everywhere—Lawrenceville's in the far stands, Stoneybrook's in the near ones.

Behind the south goalpost, the scoreboard looked like this:

Stoneybrook   Lawrenceville

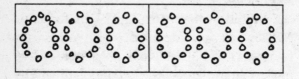

"This is so cool!" Mary Anne squealed.

"Nifty set-up," Richard said.

We went straight to the signing-in booth. The woman there gave us a long timetable of events. She signed us up for tug-of-war, the baton relay and the sack race.

"What about the underwear race?" I asked.

Mum gave Richard a Look. He cleared his throat and said, "Yes, well, I'm afraid I put the kibosh on that one."

"He refused to come unless we substituted something else," Mum explained.

"Maybe next year." Richard's face was turning red just talking about it.

"What's a kibosh?" I asked Mary Anne as we walked to the stands.

"A Dad word," she said. "It means to say no to something."

"Dawn! Mary Anne!" Kristy's voice shouted from the stands.

"Hi!" Mary Anne yelled back. My family

climbed up the rows of benches and found seats next to the Brewer/Thomases.

"I'm so excited!" Kristy announced. "We're doing the home run derby, the three-legged race . . ."

I should probably explain "Run for Your Money" in more detail. It was divided into two parts. The first half consisted of the more usual events, the second half of the weird ones (including the ones the BSC had entered). Many events ran at the same time, with referees for each one. Each team scored two points for a win, one for a tie and none for a loss. The refs kept scoreboards, and "runners" circulated the field, collecting the cards to bring to the master scorekeeper.

The Schafer/Spier events were in the first half, beginning with the tug-of-war. We played against a family called the Medallises, from Lawrenceville. They also had two eighth-grade girls.

"Everybody here?" asked the referee, who was the owner of a music shop at the local mall.

"Yes, sir," Mr Medallis said, picking up one end of the rope. Then he looked at us with a smile. "You ready to be beaten silly?"

One of the girls rolled her eyes. "*Da-ad!*"

"We'll see about that!" Richard answered. "Come on."

Oh, well, boys will be boys.

"Ready . . . steady . . . go!" the ref said.

The Medallises were strong—but we were stronger. "Pullll!" Mum grunted. *"Pulllll!"*

We lurched backward. The Medallises fell to the ground in a heap.

"The winners—the Schafer/Spiers!" the ref called out. "Two points, Stoneybrook."

We hugged each other. We had won two of the first points that day! Then Mary Annc insisted we shake hands with the other family. (What a good sport!)

We celebrated our victory by buying some drinks at a stand. We said hello to the Newtons, the Barretts and about a million other people. Then we watched Kristy's family win a three-legged race, and the Kishis lose a relay race. Before long the scoreboard said Stoneybrook 24, Lawrenceville 8. Yea!

Next we ran the sack race. Our opponent was this incredibly enthusiastic family, the Smiths, who had a boy and a girl. As soon as we met them, one of the boys said, "Are you really sisters? You don't even look alike."

I don't know why that bothered me, but it did. Mary Anne cheerfully explained that we were a stepfamily, and the race began.

106

We lost that one. The baton relay was next, and we lost that, too. Mary Anne was very good-natured about it. She kept on saying, "I'm just glad Dad and I have won *anything*."

But our mood had sunk a little, and Mum could tell.

"Hey, how about some pinball, Dawn?" she asked.

"Okay."

As we walked to the sideshows, I looked around at the crowd. I wondered how many other people were part of stepfamilies. I saw a lot of look-alike siblings.

Everyone seemed somehow more . . . warm and excited than we did. I kept telling myself that was ridiculous, but it wasn't.

I knew why, too. They were real families. They knew they were going to live together, year in and year out. Not partial families, with one member going away for months at a time. I had one foot in Stoneybrook and the other in Palo City. No wonder we lost. I was pulling us apart.

I felt an awful twisty sensation in my stomach. How can you love two separate families and not feel like an outcast, or a traitor?

One thing was for sure. I needed a good game of pinball.

I took a peep at the scoreboard as Mum and I started to play. It looked like this:

Stoneybrook   Lawrenceville

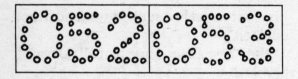

Suddenly I couldn't wait for the BSC events to start.

12th CHAPTER

"And then Becca decided her trainers were too tight, just as the referee yelled, 'Go!'" Jessi said.

It was half time at "Run for Your Money". The score was now Stoneybrook 97, Lawrenceville 94. All seven of us regular BSC members had decided to get together and buy our lunch at a stand. Everyone had a crazy story to tell about her family's events. Jessi's saga was about the triathlon.

"So Becca just *sat* there, screaming 'Do it again, do it again!'" Jessi went on. "But she wouldn't wear the trainers, and Daddy wouldn't let her run in bare feet. Well, she sulked for about an *hour*, till we entered Squirt in the baby race. *He* wouldn't go in the right direction, because he kept wanting to hug Becca. He felt sorry for her."

"That's so sweet!" Stacey said.

"Remember the rolling race we practised?" Mal asked. "Well, Adam refused to do it with Jordan because he was too embarrassed to hold hands."

We groaned.

"I thought my family had done really well in the three-legged race," Kristy said, "until Mum noticed that David Michael had used one of her silk scarves as a binding. Was she angry!"

We walked from stand to stand, talking and laughing. Each time we stopped, everyone looked at Stacey and me to see if the food would be all right for our "diets".

Do you know what it's like to be a vegetarian surrounded by nothing but hot dogs, hamburgers, sausage and fried chicken? Torture!

At last we found a stand that sold corn on the cob and bags of peanuts. I was still full from our power breakfast, so that was okay.

As we wandered over to the sideshows, Mr Kishi called out, "Hello, girls!" He and Mrs Kishi were playing table football against Janine. Honestly, I'd never seen that girl move so fast. She was grabbing those knobs as if her life depended on it, shouting and laughing and having a wonderful time.

We looked at Claudia. She smiled and shrugged. "The girl's crazy. I always knew there was an animal hiding inside her."

Just as we sat down in the stands, a voice boomed out, "Attention, please. Will everyone take their places for the second half of 'Run for Your Money'!"

We checked our list. In five minutes we were scheduled for the dance relay race.

By one of the goalposts, an official was inserting a cassette into a huge tape deck with twin speakers. We met our Lawrenceville opponents, seven girls about our age.

The referee was this prim old woman, who said, "Stoneybrook is Lane One, and Lawrenceville is Lane Two. You'll see six orange markers ahead of you in each lane, one for each teammate in the relay. If anyone drops the baton, the team is disqualified. Now, we're going to play a pretty fast tune, so you can really *boogie down*."

We burst into giggles at that. Then we took our marks. Kristy was first in the relay, I was second, then Mary Anne, Stacey, Mal, Claudia and Jessi.

When the ref said, "Go!" a rock dance tune started blaring. Kristy froze. Her face went red as a beetroot.

The girl on the other team was gyrating down the track, her hair swinging back and forth. Her teammates were doubled over laughing.

Well, Kristy may have been embarrassed, but she was also losing. And Kristy hates to lose.

She began hopping down the track, somehow moving her legs forward very fast. She looked . . . well, dorky would be an understatement. *We* were all cracking up.

I was next. Let me tell you, it's hard to run and dance at the same time—especially when you feel like a complete idiot. Crowds were forming on the sidelines, howling at us. I could see Jamie Newton staring in shock, as if something was wrong with us.

The teams were neck-and-neck to the last dancer. That's where we had our secret weapon—Jessi Ramsey, star ballerina.

You should have seen her. She did these incredible spinning leaps (*tour jetés*, she called them). The other girl stopped and gaped in amazement.

"The winner is Stoneybrook!" the referee called out.

"Yea, Jessi!" We crowded around her for a group hug. One of the Lawrenceville girls came over and started asking Jessi about her dance classes.

After they put our score up, the scoreboard read Stoneybrook 99, Lawrenceville 98.

Mondo Ball was a few events away. We watched the Papadakis team lose the basketball shooting contest. We half-expected Linny to throw a tantrum, but instead Hannie started to cry—and Linny *comforted* her.

Some other highlights: the Barretts won a game of leapfrog, but Buddy hit his head on a goalpost while dancing around in triumph. One of the Pike teams won at water balloon hot potato, after spraying the referee. The Arnolds lost the underwear race, mostly because they were laughing too hard; and Charlotte's dog, Carrot, escaped from a pet race to chase after a squirrel.

Stoneybrook was behind 113–112 when Mondo Ball was announced. We ran out to the field and watched a team of four grown-ups roll this unbelievable *thing* towards us. It was more like a barrage balloon than a ball.

"Are we sure we want to do this?" Claudia asked.

"Where's your team spirit?" Kristy replied.

"That thing's going to swallow us up!" Mal cried.

"Okay, teams, line up on either side of the Mondo Ball!" the referee called out.

It was now or never. We stood in the shadow of this two-metre high globe.

"Ready . . . steady . . . go!"

Well, you don't *know* what trying to move that thing was like. If you pushed it, your hands sunk in to it, so you had to throw your body against it. Then, if the people on the other side pushed harder than you, the ball would sort of glom over you.

Mondo Ball bounced and skidded and glommed up and down the field. It was impossible to get control of it. Half the time neither team even knew which direction we were going. At one point Stacey jumped on it and rolled all the way over the top.

Somehow we manoeuvred the ball over to the Lawrenceville side. I think it was luck, but Kristy insists we did it on our own.

The referee blew a whistle. "Points to Stoneybrook!"

"Yeeee-hah!" Kristy shouted.

We were thrilled. Two events, two victories. Immediately Mondo Ball became a crowd favourite. (After us, teams were lining up to play for the rest of the afternoon.)

We stuck together till the end, cheering on our friends and playing on the sideshow games. Kristy even managed to hand out a couple of BSC leaflets (can you believe it?). At one point, Logan turned up and hung around with us. (He'd had to work that day, at his part-time waiter's job.)

The last event ended at five o'clock sharp. Then the announcer said: "Ladies and gentlemen, we are now awaiting the final tally. The runners are handing in the scoreboards, and the official scorer is adding everything up. If you'll bear with us . . ."

The noise level dropped. You could hear leaves rustling in the breeze. We were all huddled together in front of the stands, BSC members and families. None of us could sit down.

Soon the numbers on the scoreboard started to flip. When they stopped, the board looked like this:

Stoneybrook   Lawrenceville

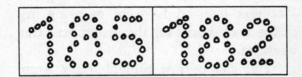

We *screamed*. Even Richard was waving his arms and yelling.

"Thank you, all participants!" the announcer continued. "The real winner of the day is Stoneybrook's chosen organization, the Housing Council, which will receive two-thirds of today's profits!"

Another big cheer went up, this time from both sides of the field.

Me? I felt *much* better than I had earlier. I hadn't had so much fun in ages.

We stood around for a few minutes, everyone laughing and talking about the events of the day. Eventually Kristy called out, "Hey, where are we going to celebrate?"

"The Rosebud Café?" Logan suggested. (That's where he works.)

We asked our parents, and they all said it was okay. It would be a pretty long walk into town, but that didn't matter. In our mood, we probably could have walked to Nova Scotia.

As we wound our way through the crowds to the pavement, Kristy spotted her maths teacher. She gasped. "Oh, my gosh! I've just realized I forgot to bring my maths book home for the assignment this weekend."

"You can borrow mine," Mary Anne said. "I'll drop it off tomorrow."

Kristy sighed with relief. "It's amazing how something like 'Run for Your Money' takes over your *life*!"

It *was* amazing. Kristy never forgets things.

A moment later Shannon Kilbourne came running towards us. "Great job on the Mondo Ball!" she called out.

"You saw us?" Stacey asked.

"Yes, I got here just in time."

We invited Shannon to the Rosebud, and

116

she got permission from her parents to come with us. Soon the nine of us began walking into town.

"You should have seen the look on your face when you rolled over that ball, Stacey," Kristy said.

"You should have seen the look on *your* face during the dance relay," Stace replied.

Kristy cringed. "That was *so* embarrassing."

"My dad said he took a picture of you," Claudia said.

"No!" Kristy's jaw dropped.

"I think I'll frame it and hang it in my room," Claud added, tapping her chin.

"You can give a print to Dawn so she can show her friends in California," Mal suggested.

"Not funny," Kristy hissed.

Everyone stopped talking, until Shannon asked, "So, are you all packed, Dawn?"

"No," I answered. "It's hard to pack for so long."

"I still can't believe you're going for six months," Logan said.

Mary Anne stood up for me. "She needs to, Logan. You don't know what it's like to have two families."

"I'd probably do the same thing if I were her," Jessi added.

"Are you lot going to be all right with just six full-time members now?" Shannon asked.

"We'll work something out," Claudia replied.

"Yes, I'm not worried." Kristy flashed me a smile. "The most important thing is for Dawn to be happy."

Whoa! Was that Kristy Thomas I was hearing? Boy, had she changed!

"Thanks, Kristy," I said. I wanted to say how much that meant to me, but I could tell she understood.

Our waiter at the restaurant was a good friend of Logan's. He led us to the best table in the place—right by the window.

One of the nice things about the Rosebud is you can talk as loudly as you want. And we did. We must have discussed every single minute of the day.

Almost everyone ordered monster sundaes. I thought Stacey would go into a diabetic coma just looking at them. (She and I ordered sane food—salad and soup.)

Soon we could see the sun setting outside the window. The buildings across the street seemed to glow with a warm amber colour.

It was a perfect end to the day. I couldn't imagine being more content.

And I began to think I was crazy for wanting to give up my life in Stoneybrook.

13th CHAPTER

Do you love *The Wizard of Oz*? I do. Sometimes I feel like Dorothy, wanting so badly to go home. Other times I feel like the Scarecrow or the Cowardly Lion.

Sunday morning was the first time I'd felt like the Tin Man.

I could hardly move. It felt as if my joints had rusted up. When I sat up, I thought I heard myself creak.

I think I must have overdone it at "Run for Your Money". I stood up carefully and hobbled across the room. Clutching the banister, I made my way downstairs.

Mary Anne was already dressed and pottering around in the kitchen. "Hi!" she said. "You look as achy as I feel."

"Uuuhhhh!" I replied, sinking into a chair. Out of the corner of my eye, I saw the oven clock. "Have I really slept till ten-thirty?"

"I've just got up myself," Mary Anne said. "What do you want for breakfast?"

"I'll get it." I shuffled over to the cupboard and grabbed the nearest packet of cereal. Mary Anne got the milk out of the fridge for me. "Where're Mum and Richard?" I asked.

"Doing errands," Mary Anne answered.

I yawned and plopped down at the table again. "I am doing *nothing* today. I don't even want to move."

Mary Anne laughed. "I know what you mean. Have you nearly finished?"

"Eating?" I replied. "Mary Anne, I've just started."

"Oh, okay. I'll wash up when you've finished . . . so you can shower and get dressed."

"Uh-huh."

"You know, I haven't seen you wear those nice cream-coloured drawstring trousers you bought last month, and that ribbed cotton T-shirt with the buttons down the front. That would look nice."

"Mm-hm."

I wondered what on earth had got into my sister. There I was, slurping cereal, my eyes half-open, looking forward to a day in which

I'd planned absolutely nothing—and Mary Anne was already dressing me.

The moment I finished my breakfast, Mary Anne took away my bowl and put it in the sink. "Er, I was rather looking forward to seconds," I said.

"Oh, sorry. Well, Dad'll be back any minute now. I think it would be nice for us to be . . . you know, dressed and ready."

"Ready? For what?"

"You know . . . for the day. That's all. I mean, he may need us to do things. The usual stuff."

I shrugged. "Yes. I suppose so."

"I was just thinking, I really adore that outfit," Mary Anne reminded me.

"Okay, okay, I'll wear it."

I began the long, *long* climb upstairs. Each step was fresh torture. When I reached the top, I was exhausted. But even though my body was a mess, my mind was waking up at last.

Something was going on. I knew it. Mary Anne *never* acted the way she'd acted at breakfast. Why did she want me to get ready so fast? How come she kept talking about that new outfit? And where were Mum and Richard, really?

I didn't need to be a genius to work out that she'd planned a surprise. That was it. People were coming over, and Mary Anne didn't want me looking like the Swamp Thing.

In the warm water of the shower, my muscles started to feel a lot better. I ran into my room and put on the outfit Mary Anne wanted. I made sure my hair was dried and combed, and I even put on a little bit of make-up.

I could hear noises downstairs. I slowed down a little. If Mary Anne was directing people into hiding places, I didn't want to spoil things.

After a few minutes, I stood up and stretched. "Oh, I feel much better!" I said loudly. "I'm all ready, Mary Anne."

"Great," Mary Anne called up.

"Here I come!"

"Okay."

I walked slowly down the stairs. Mary Anne smiled and said, "You look fabulous!"

I walked nonchalantly into the dining room. No one was there. I wandered into the living room and the family room. Empty. No one behind sofas or under tables.

Mary Anne was tidying up the house, not saying a word.

Ding-dong.

The doorbell! They were waiting outside, ready to come in. "Shall I get it?" I asked.

"If you want," Mary Anne replied.

With my biggest smile, I flung the door open.

It was Richard. Alone. "'Morning," he said. "I'm back."

I looked over his shoulder. I expected to see heads popping up from behind bushes.

Wrong.

"Any volunteers to accompany me on a dangerous mission to the grocer's?" Richard asked.

Mary Anne came into the living room. "Great," she said. "We weren't doing anything."

We walked out to the car. I began to feel excited again. Of course! They were *taking* me to a party.

Minutes later, Richard pulled up at our destination.

The grocer's.

We bought some detergent and paper towels and canned tuna fish. Then we left.

I sank into the back seat of my car. In my drawstring trousers, I was sure I had looked smashing in the household goods aisle. Ho-hum!

"Didn't you want to drop off something at Kristy's?" Richard asked Mary Anne.

"Oh! Right, the maths book she forgot!" Mary Anne said. She reached into the glove compartment. "I put it in here yesterday, just so I wouldn't forget—and then I forgot."

Richard drove across town. He pulled into the drive of the Brewer mansion. "Try not to chat for too long," Richard said. "Sharon'll be home soon."

"I'll stay in the car," I said.

"No, come on," Mary Anne insisted. "Kristy will want to see you."

Blink. The light went on in my mind. *This* was the party. They were waiting behind Kristy's front door. The maths book was just a trick.

Mary Anne rang the bell, and Kristy answered straight away. "Hi!" she said. "Hey, thanks for the book. I can't believe I forgot it."

The house was empty behind her, and quiet. No decorations, no nothing.

But it was okay. I could deal with it. I was a big girl.

"Oh!" Kristy suddenly said. "You won't believe the size of the marrow Watson found in the vegetable garden! Want to take a look?"

"Okay," Mary Anne and I replied. See? All was not lost. Maybe I wasn't getting a party, but at least I'd get to see a very large vegetable.

Kristy led us through the huge house and

out of the back door. I walked through it, stifling a yawn.

"*SURPRIIIIIISE!*"

The yawn caught in my throat. My mouth froze in the open position.

A flash went off, blinding me. Great! Someone had taken a photo of me, looking like Monstro the Whale.

When my eyes cleared, I could see a crowd of smiling faces. Stacey, Claudia, Jessi, Mal, Logan and Shannon were there, as well as a whole crowd of our charges: the Pike, Barrett, Newton, and Papadakis kids, and Charlotte Johanssen.

"Like the decorations?" Suzi Barrett asked. "I was on the committee."

"They're *beautiful*!" I said.

They were, too. A banner that said BON VOYAGE, DAWN! hung from Kristy's huge maple tree. Two picnic tables were laid with homemade California-theme centrepieces made of odds and ends and one was a plane and the other was a round face with sunglasses. On the back wall of the house, the kids had put up a mural. The scene was a beach, with a blonde girl lazing in the sun and writing letters. On the sand next to her were envelopes, and on each one was written the name of one of my charges. Across the top was written *WE LOVE YOU, DAWN! PLEASE WRITE!*

126

"That's your going-away gift," Charlotte said to me. "We know just how to fold it so you can take it with you."

I looked at Mary Anne. For the first time in our lives I started crying first.

Then Vanessa decided to read her poem. Well, let me tell you, Kristy's lawn didn't need any watering after that. I started hugging everyone left and right. The kids stared at us blankly.

"Okay, enough mushy stuff," Jordan Pike said. "Time for blindman's buff!"

Guess who was the blind man? Yours truly. The games committee had really done its work. We played Pinning the Tail on the Donkey, Red Light Green Light and Twister. Some of the kids disappeared inside for video games, but Watson chased them back out.

All the time, Buddy kept asking Kristy, "Is it time for the cake yet?"

At last Kristy could take it no longer. She, Buddy, Margo, Nicky and Claire went into the kitchen. First Claire came out with a huge tray full of chocolate chip cookies. Then Buddy proudly displayed the cake, which was roughly the shape of a haystack and the colour of mud. Its icing had been applied in thick globs.

"Yummmm!" the kids squealed.

Margo then appeared with bags of crisps

and pretzels, and Kristy brought out a punch bowl. Last came Nicky, who beamed as he held up the tofu-rhubarb pie. "Kristy said you'd like this best of all!" he announced.

"Oh, I will!" I replied. "I can't wait to eat it!"

As the kids crowded on to the benches, I began pouring drinks.

"Uh-uh-uh!" Logan said, waving me away. "You're the guest of honour."

I sat down with my tofu-rhubarb pie. A piece of chocolate icing flew past me from left to right. Buddy spat out a flake of garlic skin they hadn't seen in the cake. Claire got up from the table, clutching my leg for balance and leaving a large brown stain on my drawstring trousers. I heard the trickle of apple juice seeping through the crack of the picnic table on to the floor. At the end of the table, Adam Pike began a burping contest that grew into an all-out war.

But you know what? It could have started snowing and I wouldn't have minded. I was on Cloud Nine.

It was a weekend I would never, never forget.

14th CHAPTER

Monday. T-minus five and counting. One more week of school, and then 'bye-'bye Stoneybrook.

Was I delirious? Was I tingling with excitement?

No. I was sitting up in bed, shaking off a night's sleep, and thinking.

Thinking about the terrific party the day before. Thinking about the great time I'd had at "Run for Your Money" and the Rosebud Café.

In five days I'd be thousands of miles from all of this.

Why?

The question kept repeating itself in my mind.

In a way, I wished I'd been having a horrible life in Stoneybrook. Maybe if my friends were awful, or if my home life was dull or if Mary Anne and I hated each other, maybe then leaving would be easy. I wouldn't be having second thoughts.

I stood up. I pulled some clothes from my chest of drawers and wardrobe. The smell of coffee wafted up from the kitchen. I could hear a newspaper rustling and my mum laughing at something Richard was saying.

Mum was acting so positive about my decision. I tried putting myself in her shoes. I would never forget the look on her face when I announced what I wanted to do. It was as if she'd aged ten years.

But since then she'd really pulled herself together. So had Mary Anne and Kristy and all my other friends. Now they were supporting me, telling me how much I needed to go.

I suppose they had no choice. They knew I was going, so they had to make the best of it. Better that than sit around feeling angry or sad. In a way, they were adjusting, that's all. Adjusting to what life would be like minus Dawn.

And they were doing a good job. *Too* good, I thought.

Okay, I hate to admit it, but it was quite *flattering* to know how everyone really felt. It showed how much they cared. You know what I was thinking then? Everyone had adjusted so well, that if I'd suddenly decided *not* to go, they'd be disappointed!

No. Ridiculous. I tried to push those feelings out of my mind. I told myself to be thankful that I was leaving one happy life and going to another. Having two families made me twice as lucky as most kids, right?

Right. I looked in my mirror and smiled away my grouchy face.

But on the way downstairs, I had to work to keep that smile going.

"Good morning," everyone said.

No one talked about my trip, and I didn't bring it up. Mary Anne left a little early for school, because she was meeting Logan first. So I wolfed down breakfast and left the house alone. I was looking forward to school, to be honest. I thought it would take my mind off my dilemma.

I was wrong. A fog had settled over Stoneybrook that morning, and I think some of it got locked in my brain. I simply couldn't concentrate. What happened at tutor time? I don't even remember going. Maths? English? Social studies? Beats me. At this rate, the teachers in Palo City were going to pack me up and send me back to Mrs Amer with *defective* stamped across my forehead.

All kinds of doubts kept flooding in, stuff I'd never thought about before. Like *Dad's*

131

point of view. I mean, think about it. My decision couldn't have been easy for him, either. Setting up life as a single person, then having Jeff return unexpectedly to his life. Having to adjust to single parenthood. Working out a happy, stable life for Jeff. At least Mum had met someone else and remarried. Dad hadn't.

Well, he hadn't *married*, that is. But he *had* been dating. And he seemed pretty serious about Carol.

That was another thing. What about Dad's social life? How was he going to feel with *two* kids around the house?

I began thinking my trip might be terribly wrong.

You can imagine my relief when school ended. I was looking forward to the BSC meeting. I knew we'd talk about the weekend, and that would be fun.

Mary Anne and I arrived early, just in time to see Shannon and Jessi practising a tap-dancing routine. (Actually, on Claudia's carpet it was more like *thud*-dancing.)

"You really have to step *into* the floor," Shannon was staying. (She goes to tap classes now and then.) "You're kind of floating. Now come on, *stamp*, step, flap, ball-change!"

"That's so hard on your shins," Jessi said. "It's not at all like ballet."

"Let me try!" Kristy stood up and began stamping around as if she were trying to kill a cockroach. Shannon and Jessi cracked up. Then Claudia and Stacey decided to try. The walls began to shake.

"What's going on up there?" Janine eventually called from her room. "Marching band practice?"

We burst into giggles. "Sorry!" Claudia yelled.

For the first time that day, my mind-fog was clearing. We settled into our usual positions—Kristy sitting on the director's chair; Claudia, Mary Anne and me on the bed; Stacey on the desk chair; and Mal, Jessi and Shannon on the floor. It was a ritual. We all did it automatically.

I was already feeling nostalgic about it. Claudia and Mary Anne would soon have a lot more room on the bed. I wondered how they felt about it. And was Shannon going to take my place? I hadn't expected her to be at the meeting. Had she changed her mind and decided to become the alternate officer?

"How's your honour society project going?" I asked her.

"Great, so far," she said. "It turns out we may not be meeting on Mondays, though, so maybe I can make it to those BSC meetings during the next two months." She shrugged. "At any rate, I'll help as much as I can."

"That's great," Mary Anne piped up. "And Logan told me today he'd try really hard to make himself available."

Kristy nodded. "Cool. I knew things would work out. I mean, this isn't perfect, but we'll do the best we can." Her eyes darted to the clock, just as it turned to 5:30. "This meeting shall come to order!"

"*Shall?*" Claudia said.

"Yes, it sounds more official," Kristy replied.

"How about saying 'cometh'," Claudia suggested. "This meeting shall cometh to order."

"Then you have to say 'Hear ye, hear ye!'" Stacey added.

"Heareth ye, heareth ye! Ye Olde Meeting of the Babysitters Club shall cometh to order!" Shannon announced.

Kristy giggled. "You lot are crazy."

I wanted to laugh. Everybody else was laughing. So I tried, but it came out sounding fake.

Why? Well, when my fog finally disappeared, something happened. All my thoughts from the day swirled together, and I could see them clearly.

When my parents had been together, I once had to make a decision. It seemed important at the time, but now I don't remember exactly what it was—whether to join a club or something. Well, Dad gave me a great suggestion. He told me to draw a line down the middle of a piece of paper and label the columns PRO and CON. I'd list reasons *to* do whatever it was in the left-hand column and reasons *not* to do it in the right-hand column. I would make my choice based on whichever list had the most items.

I was doing that in my head now. On the PRO side, for going to California, I listed these things:

1. Being with Dad and Jeff.
2. Seeing my old friends.
3. Being in California.

On the CON side:

1. Missing Mum.
2. Missing Mary Anne.
3. Missing the Babysitters Club.
4. Coming back to find the BSC didn't really need me after all.
5. Doing terribly in my new school.
6. Doing terribly when I come back to SMS.
7. Not getting along with Carol.
8. Putting too much pressure on Dad.
9. Having the kind of experience Jessi had in Oakley.

The list went on and on. But I didn't finish it. I didn't have to. A decision had planted itself in my brain. I couldn't believe I hadn't come to it earlier.

I had to announce it straight away. Claudia and Mary Anne were in the middle of scheduling a sitting job for the next week, and they were having a hard time.

"Er, listen everyone," I said. "Don't worry about not scheduling me. Go ahead if you need to."

Claudia shook her head. "It's for a week from Thursday. You won't be here—unless you want to fly back to sit for the Prezziosos."

"I won't need to," I said. "I'm not going."

Claudia dropped the receiver. She quickly picked it up and said into it: "Er, can I call you back? . . . Thanks, 'bye." *Click.* She hung up and stared at me. "*Whaaaaat?*"

"I'm staying here. I've changed my mind."

The room was so quiet I could swear I heard the sun setting. I began laughing. "Well . . . say something!"

"Are you sure?" Mary Anne asked.

"Mm-hm."

"Who-o-oa!" Kristy said under her

breath. A smile began flickering across her face.

Claudia let out a whooshing breath. "Okay, who's going to organize the Welcome Back party?"

Well, the meeting turned to chaos. Claudia went rummaging around for all the junk food she could find. Mary Anne grabbed a box of tissues and began wiping tears away. My friends asked me questions, but not many. I think they were afraid that if I thought about my decision too much, I might change my mind.

But the lists had made it clear. The score was at least twelve cons to three pros. I was staying.

At the end of the meeting, Mary Anne and I raced to our bikes. As we rode home, I thought and thought about my one remaining problem.

Breaking the news to my parents.

15th CHAPTER

A tear fell on to my book. There was only one word on the page, at the top: *JOURNAL*. I'd written it in bold letters, with a felt-tip pen. I'd never kept a journal before, so I wanted to make a definite, strong statement. Now the ink on the letter *L* was all smudged, and the page was starting to pucker up.

Oh, well. I suppose a journal's meant to be about feelings, and I'll always know what the tear was about.

I tried looking out of the window, but the setting sun was too strong. Instead I sat back. My stomach was growling and churning, and suddenly I wished I hadn't eaten that huge plate of ravioli for dinner.

I was going to be getting another dinner soon, anyway.

Bing! A bell chimed, followed by a soft

voice. "Good evening, folks. I'm Captain Jordan, and on behalf of the entire flight crew, I'd like to welcome you to trans-continental flight six-six-two to Los Angeles. We've been cleared for take-off, so we're about to taxi on to the runway. The skies are looking pretty clear . . ."

This was it. I shielded my eyes and looked out of the window again. This time I could make out the silhouettes of Mum, Richard and Mary Anne against a window in the airport, staring at the plane. I waved, but they didn't see me.

Now my tears were dripping on to the handrest. Someone stirred in the seat next to me, but I didn't turn my head. I wanted to be alone with my thoughts. I had just spent the longest, toughest week of my life.

Okay. Let me begin at the beginning. I suppose that means Monday, after the BSC meeting.

I was sure I'd come to my final decision. Mary Anne and I got home in record time. I called an emergency family meeting during dinner, and Mary Anne sat next to me at the table.

Patiently I described my pro-and-con list to Mum and Richard. I apologized for messing up their plans and waffling back and forth, but my mind was made up. I wasn't going to California.

Mum nodded and smiled. The first thing she said was, "Darling, sometimes a decision like this can't be made by counting things on a list."

"But it was so lopsided," I said.

"I know," she replied. "But not each item is equally important."

Richard nodded. "Besides, you listed the pros and cons of moving to California. But you didn't list the pros and cons of staying in Stoneybrook."

Well, I exploded at that. "It sounds as if you *want* me to go!"

"Oh, no! No, darling, that's not it at all," Mum said. She sighed deeply, and her eyes began to water. "The list was a great idea. It shows how deeply you've been thinking about this. But I know you, Dawn. I know when you're speaking from your heart and when you're speaking from your brain."

She didn't need to say any more. My anger started to melt into a little pool and trickle away. Mum was right. My poor little heart had been working overtime for weeks. The list had been a way to give it a rest and let my brain do the work.

Only Mum could see that. It must have been so hard for her to have to persuade me to go. But she knew if I let the list make my decision, I'd regret it. "I suppose we might eventually have the same problem again, huh?" I said.

Mum shrugged and looked down sadly, and I thought about how much I loved her.

Next to me, Mary Anne was soaking a tissue. Even Richard had tears in his eyes. All week long I'd been wondering whether everyone really cared about me. I wasn't wondering any more.

Our meeting lasted way past dinnertime. I began to talk once again about the reasons I was aching to go to California. That's what it was, an ache. And I realized it would have been impossible to cover it up.

That night I rang my friends, one by one. They sounded sad, but I think they were kind of expecting my news. They'd scheduled me for one job the next week, but Kristy assured me she could cover it.

The rest of the week I packed and said lots of goodbyes. I went shopping with Claudia and Stacey for new clothes. I had second (third? fourth?) thoughts, but not once did I change my mind again. Then on Friday I had a meeting with Mrs Amer, who made me feel confident I'd do all right in my new school.

I took a mental picture of SMS as I left

it on Friday afternoon, but I didn't say goodbye. *It'll be here in six months*, I thought, *barring an earthquake*. Thinking that made me laugh. I really am such a Californian.

At our Friday meeting BSC might as well have stood for the Bawlers and Sniffers Club. We could hardly answer the phone. Claudia must have told four different parents she had a cold.

On our final bike ride home, I thought Mary Anne and I would both topple over. It's hard to see the street when your eyes are wet.

Between last-minute packing and shopping, Friday night and Saturday flew by. Late in the afternoon, the doorbell rang. I ran to open it, with Mary Anne behind me.

Jessi, Mal, Kristy, Stacey and Claudia were standing on the porch. They were dressed beautifully, holding out a wrapped present.

"Oh, you *didn't*!" I said. (Honestly, I don't how a person's body can keep producing so many tears. I thought mine would have been used up by then, but *no*.)

"We did," Claudia said.

"Shall I open it?" I asked.

"Yes," Mal said. "You'll need it on the plane."

I ripped open the wrapping and the box. Inside was a gorgeous, leather-bound book of blank pages.

I gasped. "I *love* it!" I said.

"It's a journal," Mallory explained. "So you can write down everything that happens."

"And then show us," Stacey added.

"We thought you might get rusty while you were away from the BSC notebook," Kristy said.

"Oh, thanks! I'll miss you lot—so—" I couldn't finish. I just threw my arms open and everyone fell into them. We must have stood there for twenty minutes, crying and hugging, and I'll-miss-you-ing.

When they left, I felt a huge tug in my stomach. But I had to think of the flight then.

Mum, Richard, Mary Anne and I piled into the car around four o'clock and drove to the Rosebud Café for dinner. Logan was working, which was wonderful. I would have felt silly crying in front of a strange waiter.

Dinner was fun, but I think we were all rather nervous about getting stuck in a traffic jam on the way to the airport. I gulped down my ravioli (which, of course, I later regretted).

We reached the airport with plenty of

time to spare, which turned out to be a bad idea. Mary Anne and I blubbered uncontrollably. Then Mum and I held on to each other as if we were permanently stuck.

You know what she whispered in my ear? Not "Write," or "Brush your teeth," or "Get good grades," or anything like that.

She said, "Let Daddy love you as much as I do."

I had to get on the plane fast before I dissolved into one huge tear.

The whole week flashed through my mind in the time it took the captain to finish his speech. As the "Fasten Your Seatbelt" sign came on, I looked out of the window again.

Mum and Richard and Mary Anne weren't there any more. I turned to my book and began writing:

JOURNAL
Saturday
It's 6:45. The sun is setting behind the airport terminal. In five hours, it will be 8:45, and I will be home...

144

I was rather surprised I'd written the word *home*. I crossed it out and wrote *in California*.

But neither one seemed exactly right. I stopped writing and stared at the words for a long time.

Then I made a decision. I'd leave it. After all, it didn't really matter. I could always go back and change it if I wanted.

Six months was a long time.

The Babysitters Club

Look out for 68

JESSI AND THE BAD BABYSITTER

"Where have you been?" Kristy demanded.

A look of bewilderment came over Wendy's face. I could see she didn't understand why Kristy had spoken so sharply. "I had a babysitting job, but the mother was late coming home," she explained. "Did any jobs come in for me?"

"There would have been if you'd been here," Kristy told her. I'm sure Wendy could see she was pretty angry. But she didn't react the way I would have. I'd have been mortified and apologetic. Wendy wasn't, though. She grew angry in return.

"What's the big deal?" she asked. "Can't Mary Anne tell from that record book thing whether or not I'm free? Why do I have to be here?"

"Because you have to be," Kristy said, her face turning pink as she held back her anger.

"We're all expected to come to every

meeting unless it's a real emergency," I explained.

"Well, this was an emergency," Wendy insisted. "I couldn't leave the kids by themselves."

"Next time call," Mary Anne said. "And why did you take a job without telling us?"

"What do you mean?" asked Wendy.

"That's the second club rule you've broken," Kristy jumped in.

"I don't know what you're talking about!" Wendy said irritably. Her hands were on her hips and I could tell she wasn't liking the treatment she was receiving from Kristy.

"First, you were late without calling, then you took a job that wasn't offered to the rest of the club." Kristy spoke coolly.

"And you saying I have to hand my regular jobs over to the club?" Wendy cried indignantly.

"We all share jobs," said Stacey. "Even if a client asks for one certain sitter, we say that we can't do that. That's the only way it will be fair."

"Okay, I can see that, I guess," Wendy conceded reluctantly. "Sorry. And next time I'll call."

Are you following the Babysitters Club Mysteries series?

Look out for:

BABYSITTERS LITTLE SISTER

Meet Karen Brewer. She's seven years old and her big sister Kristy runs the Babysitters Club. And Karen's always having adventures of her own . . . Read all about her in her very own series.

The Babysitters Club

Need a babysitter? Then call the Babysitters Club. Kristy Thomas and her friends are all experienced sitters. They can tackle any job from rampaging toddlers to a pandemonium of pets. To find out all about them, read on!

No 37: **Dawn and the Older Boy**
No 38: **Kristy's Mystery Admirer**
No 39: **Poor Mallory!**
No 40: **Claudia and the Middle School Mystery**
No 41: **Mary Anne vs. Logan**
No 42: **Jessi and the Dance School Phantom**
No 43: **Stacey's Emergency**
No 44: **Dawn and the Big Sleepover**
No 45: **Kristy and the Baby Parade**
No 46: **Mary Anne Misses Logan**
No 47: **Mallory on Strike**
No 48: **Jessi's Wish**
No 49: **Claudia and the Genius of Elm Street**
No 50: **Dawn's Big Date**
No 51: **Stacey's Ex-Best Friend**
No 52: **Mary Anne and Too Many Babies**
No 53: **Kristy for President**
No 54: **Mallory and the Dream Horse**
No 55: **Jessi's Gold Medal**
No 56: **Keep Out, Claudia!**
No 57: **Dawn Saves the Planet**
No 58: **Stacey's Choice**
No 59: **Mallory Hates Boys (and Gym)**
No 60: **Mary Anne's Makeover**
No 61: **Jessi and the Awful Secret**
No 62: **Kristy and the Worst Kid Ever**
No 63: **Claudia's Friend Friend**
No 64: **Dawn's Family Feud**
No 65: **Stacey's Big Crush**
No 66: **Maid Mary Anne**

Look out for:

No 68: **Jessi and the Bad Babysitter**
No 69: **Get Well Soon, Mallory!**
No 70: **Stacey and the Cheerleaders**

Goosebumps

by R.L. Stine

Reader beware, you're in for a scare!

These terrifying tales will send shivers up your spine . . .

Available now:

Look out for:

Animal Rescue by Bette Paul

Tessa finds life in the country *so* different from life in
the town. Will she ever be accepted? But everything
changes when she meets Nora and Ned who run the
village animal sanctuary, and becomes involved in a
struggle to save the badgers of Delves Wood
from destruction . . .

Thunderfoot by Deborah van der Beek

Mel Whitby has always loved horses, and when she
comes across an enormous but neglected horse in a
railway field, she desperately wants to take care of it.
But little does she know that taking care of
Thunderfoot will change her life forever . . .

A Foxcub Named Freedom
by Brenda Jobling

A vixen lies seriously injured in the undergrowth. Her
young son comes to her for comfort and warmth. The
cub wants to help his mother to safety, but it is
impossible. The vixen, sensing danger, nudges him
away, caring nothing for herself – only for
his freedom . . .